Surfing the C.I.A.

by
Nicholas Ware

pince-nez press
san francisco

Surfing the C.I.A.
© 2003 Nicholas Ware
Printed in the U.S.A.
ISBN 1-930074-09-3
Library of Congress Catalog Card No. 2003102185

Cover design, page design, and layout: Idintdoit Design
Fonts: Janson Text, Avant Garde, ITC Luna

All rights reserved. No part of this book may be reproduced in any form or by any electronic means, including information storage and retrieval systems, without permission from the publisher except by a reviewer who may quote brief passages in a review.

This is a work of fiction; any resemblance to actual events or to persons living or dead, exists only in the imagination of the reader, and is purely coincidental.

The publisher gratefully acknowledges the assistance of those who helped with this book: Bill Vogel, Donna Vogel, Robin Sterns, Ph.D., and Kim Burgess.

Pince-Nez Press
San Francisco, CA
(415) 267-5978 fax (800) 579-3614
www.pince-nez.com
info@pince-nez.com

This work of fiction is dedicated to people everywhere who oppose war,

and

to all my friends, regardless of what they think.

Nicholas Ware
Coconut Grove, Florida
February, 2003

Indonesia

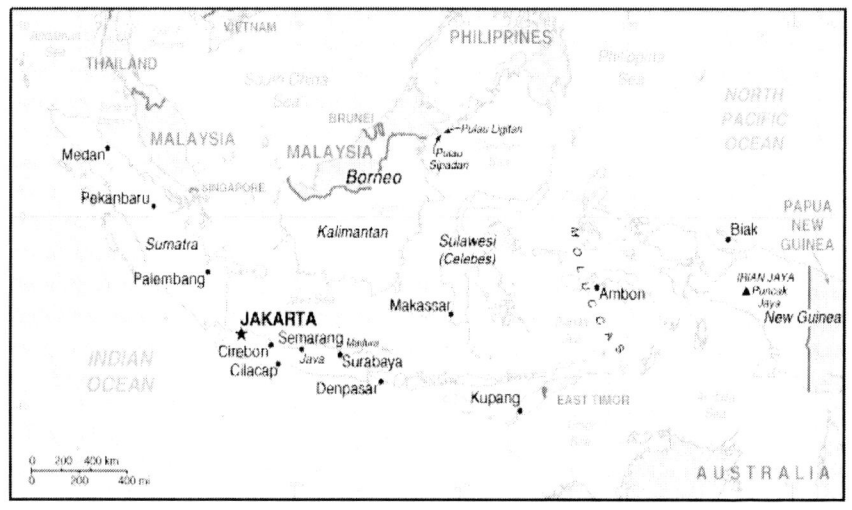

Reprinted without permission from C.I.A.
The World Factbook, Indonesia, 2003
www.cia.gov/cia/publications/factbook/geos/id.html

Prologue

Jakarta. Traffic. Fragrances of wood smoke, exhaust and cloves, mixed with incense and cooking oil. Traffic. Blue smoke rises from a horde of motorbikes as they grind out into the boulevard in a black mass, helmets hanging from handlebars, and weave around one another in the crowd of green taxis and bikes and trucks overflowing with people and bundles. A thick milk chocolate brown canal pulsates by the side of the road. Air bubbles appear in its surface where a man wades chest deep in the warm brown liquid. No wind stirs the eucalyptus along the banks. Colored cloth *topis*, the black *peci* caps that comprise the uniform of Indonesian officialdom and of Islam, appear, bobbing in the throng. Drivers and lifters sweat, everyone working, everyone active. A blind man sells pencils on the rusty iron flyover; on the steps a few belts are laid out on a cloth. In the shade, a man sits crosslegged, studying a chessboard; another sips coffee, squatting on the dark, bare earth. The sky is white and burning over Jakarta and the city is dirty and always active, with prayer just a few hours away, and the chance to wash one's arms and feet and move to the calm and cool of the mosque. In the neighborhoods, a taste of old Djakarta, the Dutch-built homes and the shaded walks hard by. Gardeners trim with machetes, chopping green grass and dark earth; all is domesticated, cultivated. Every square meter has been stepped over and trod upon; the weight of the people of Java is felt here. By sheer numbers of them, no place is left for snakes or unwanted pests. Cats, winnowy creatures, move freely as though somehow spared, but they are harmless and clean. Dogs are shooed away, chased or stoned by the devout: the animals are known to carry disease, unless they belong to a rich man, or a *buleh*, foreigner, albino. But the first thing, for sure, is the traffic.

Chapter One

The year was 1990 and I was a newly minted but fully certified Central Intelligence Agency Operations Officer. I had just completed the yearlong career training program, the Agency's dating service, and was now awaiting assignment. Hanging around. On this Wednesday, I found myself sitting at a lunch table in the sterile cafeteria of "Langley," CIA headquarters in McLean, Virginia, surrounded by linoleum, waiting for this guy named Brian Stokes, who had just come out of three years in Jakarta, Indonesia, in position x-7. I was awaiting assignment to job x-7. For many officers, this assignment would look like a waste of time at best. It was a Third World tour in a nation whose trade with the U.S. was less than fifteen percent of its GNP, and so it was unimportant from an economic point of view. It was also unimportant from a strategic point of view, as it had a stable military dictatorship, considered benign under the American analysis, and there was just not that much to report there. From the Agency's perspective, Jakarta had been a place to target cold war recruitments, but even that was fading as the spirit of Glasnost spread through the Soviet Bloc and satellites of Russia became democracies selling Levi's.

Of course nobody was thinking of surf but me. From that perspective, this assignment was beyond my wildest dreams. I was hoping to get to Mexico or Peru, but I had managed to come up with Indo, partially by accident, and this was my ticket to surf heaven. This dude Stokes was no surfer. I could tell that just by reading his operational cables as they came across the Indonesia desk in East Asia Division at Langley. He wrote in a standard, acceptable way but his prose contained too much effort; the need to conform. There was no lazy glide to his writing, no risks taken, no departure from the norm. Like so much around me, it had a deadening effect on me, and killed the romance of the spying game.

The ceiling fans whirred, nearly noiselessly. People bustled around with their trays, pairing off at the clean, slick tables. I watched the bearded analysts sitting together discussing Bulgarian rooftops or whatever they talk about, took in sounds from the kitchen, cash registers, people eating. Someone dropped a fork. The cafeteria had recently been organized to match the food court look of an American shopping mall with kiosk-type service replacing the old cafeteria look. Burgers, sushi, what have you. Where the hell was Stokes, and how did all these people get so fat?

Stokes arrived, twenty minutes late, important, formal, the young executive whose time is in demand. He had an air that said, "I am a professional; I have many appointments; my dance card is full; I carry an electronic agenda." He brought to my mind a pro baseball player being interviewed in the locker room after winning the big one. This impression was so strong that I would forever picture Stokes wearing a towel around his neck, like a locker room ballplayer, his hair wet from a shower, earnestly speaking into a sports reporter's mike. What Stokes was saying was very clear: "I outrank you."

Stokes had done well in Jakarta. He had completed what they call a successful tour. When he left he took full credit for his success, thanked nobody, and went off to his next posting, no doubt the next of many in a successful career.

I would get nothing out of Stokes, other than what I gleaned from the questions he asked me. First was, "Do you play golf?" I shook my head no.

"Tennis?"

"Mmm'mm."

"Softball? We have an embassy league." His voice rose.

I told him I knew how to play, but my last softball game was on the Capitol Mall with my cover classmates from the Foreign Service Institute and not particularly athletic; the fact was, although I didn't feel at liberty to say so, or at liberty to say much of anything in this first encounter with this incredibly conventional guy, I felt like I was getting out of shape since I hadn't been surfing. Even though the Paramilitary Course I took in training had been physical, it wasn't the same as paddling every morning, and only a surfer knows what it takes out of you to paddle through whitewater.

My mind drifted to a morning session at a spot called Davenport Landing in Northern California where the water was crystal smooth and there was something delicate in the way the waves folded as they broke . . . something feminine and yielding in those crisp blue cylinders . . . . But then I looked up to see Mr. Stokes studying me. I must have looked pretty spaced out, reflecting on a long ago surf session three thousand miles away.

From the look Stokes was giving me though, I could tell he meant something serious, so I figured we were going to get down to a substantive intelligence topic, and we did: The Embassy League. As I glazed over again, I could hear him warming to his topic. Fond memories of trouncing an oil company team in softball, of soccer games that became tools for meeting Russian diplomats, and everything about who plays what game at what field in Jakarta, until I felt like blurting out that I thought that was great but what about Indonesia, did anyone ever even venture into it? What about the islands I had been reading about all my life in the surf rags? What about Bali or Pulau Nias, the famous right break off the north coast?

Then my mind went back to my preadolescence, when a kid's worth was judged by his baseball skills, and parents pushed their kids and I was never much good and played left field if anything. For a moment, the sadness of those days intruded into my thoughts, just as the Davenport Landing session had and I was seeing myself plodding to school in a much-too big baseball uniform with the words Mutual of Omaha sewn on the back.

All of this went through my head in flashes as I sat across the linoleum table from Brian Stokes in the cafeteria at Langley, with the neon lights shining down from high up on the ceiling and autumn leaves blowing around in the quad, and when I kind of awakened from my rhapsody Brian Stokes was studying me again. It was clear by this time that he had no more use for me than I had for him, with the difference being that he still outranked me. But not being a totally bad guy, he showed me some charity now.

Stokes looked at me and said, "But you look like you work out. I mean you seem to be in pretty good shape. What kind of sports are you into?" The question seemed to presuppose that the list of sports he had asked me about was exhaustive, the only sports in the world. He had a quizzical look, as though it were germane, and not only that, but essential to my qualifications for the assignment.

"I'm a surfer," I said. Brian Stokes looked directly at me for a long moment, his expression blank. Then he leaned back his head and rolled his eyes.

I spent the next two weeks, the last prior to my departure, mostly trying to predict what my experience would be like. I had a lot in the way of last minute tasks at headquarters, and I got to parts of the building I had never been in before, where the elevators were different colors than the ones I was used to in my division, but everything else was more or less uniform. I thought a lot about my conversation with Stokes. He was what he was, but then so was I; but he had me wondering about the people I would be working with in the Station.

Surfers are driven by places more than people, and it was dawning on me that this was not going to be just a trip to a palm-studded archipelago with waves everywhere. It is dangerous to anticipate a place when you have never been there, especially if the place is Asia with its vastness and cultural mix. I was ready for meeting locals, just like anywhere I had traveled, mainly to surf, but I was getting the message now that it was the Americans who would be more intimately involved with me, and that was a bit of a worry. Was Stokes telling me that I would be judged by my ability in sports like golf and softball? What was up with that? I was going to a country where the national sport was badminton. If I were headed off to Spain, would we be playing golf on the day of the bullfights? Not only that, but what's wrong with surfing? It's not a team sport. Maybe that was it.

That year a wonderful bar had opened in Arlington, Virginia, called Strangeways, after the brewery. It was a funky spot full of spikes and leather with murals on the walls and green hair and great girls and beer. It wasn't much like the yuppie spots we frequented when we were going through training, so I could get away there and get some normalcy, California style.

Surfing the C.I.A.

The chick behind the bar, Nadia, was way ahead of her time. She had henna in her hair and olive skin and a hummingbird tattooed on her wrist, and when you asked her for a beer, she just stared at you and *then* gave you a beer. Someone like that could mean a lot to me, and I drank a number of beers just to go through that routine, to speak to her and get her response, which was always identical. Something in that ritual was tremendously comforting for a person whose world was in flux. I wondered what it would be like to spend my life with such a funky girl and how it would fit with what I was doing. Obviously she wouldn't know I was CIA, or maybe that is the kind of thing silent-beer-pouring girls just figure out.

I had had a girlfriend, but we were split up and there was nobody around just now and this girl who dressed like a witch was very appealing. Girls like that make their own choices, however, and I would have to just see what she did.

My last girlfriend, Chary, was a much more yuppie type, although not entirely yuppie inside. She was a Foreign Service Officer from the A-100 course and we had taken up together on a weekend training exercise in Harper's Ferry, where a hotel served as an embassy and we were all its diplomats. It was one of those exercises where everyone plays a role so you get to know who is who in a genuine embassy, and it worked, more or less. Anyway, after the course and some great sex on the roof of the hotel in Harper's Ferry, she had gone off to Europe, and I had gone into language training, and that was pretty much that. She was my girlfriend for only a month.

I had no problem at all bridging the funkiness/yuppie gap between these two, and it occurred to me how easily a man can consider a broad range of women in the same light. I could remember looking at Chary the same way I was now viewing Nadia, and wondering in the same way how she would fit into my life. On the other hand, you could just see Nadia on a tropical beach in a sarong, whereas Chary had been more of an erotic type who liked power and business and government and also liked very much being screwed in strange places, attributes which frequently go hand in hand.

With a woman like Nadia, the question was how to best proceed, or, in her vernacular, how to bust a move. The fact is there was no good way. You could wait for her when she got off work, but that was pretty lame if she didn't respond well to it. You could be very bold and let her know how you were feeling, but that also could be pretty lame if she didn't respond well to it. So it was really up to her. You could send her some signals, but she would have to take it upon herself to cross the distance between you, and that put her in the position of potentially feeling lame rather than you—shifting the burden.

Nadia was more of a Seattle girl than a DC girl. She was a painter, a good one. The murals in Strangeways were all her work and she had lots of canvases at home. In Arlington, not the most artistic town, she was a little bit displaced. But people with talent always find their place eventually; I imagined she would end up in Greenwich Village or LA.

Surfing the C.I.A.

When it happened between us, she busted the sweetest move I ever saw. I had pretty much abandoned the possibility of anything happening, and had resigned myself to worshipping her from afar, as you do with so many women along the way. This night she was wearing her cool black leather jacket and her face looked slightly different. I finally figured out she had made herself up just a bit. Her lips were red and glossy, nearly severe, but her olive complexion and that henna with her smooth skin were the right tones against each other—strangely mixed, fantastic. They gave her overall a foreign glow, a Moorish quality, a dark countenance.

I went to the bar and asked her for a beer. For the first time, a faint smile crossed her face, revealing two rows of strong, white teeth. At that moment, she looked so beautiful that I nearly turned away from her. I actually considered walking out of the bar and never coming back. I didn't know what to say, but fortunately my body had taken command, and at least I found that I was smiling at her. Her smile kept growing and she began to laugh slightly, and I did as well, and in seconds we were both laughing together at the end of the bar. The music, always funky and backbeat solid '80s New Wave punk, was pounding a bass out of Depeche Mode: "Your own . . . personal . . . Jesus . . ." and Nadia's hand was delicately upon my shoulder, so lightly that I could not even feel it through my shirt. Her other hand was at my waist, and I felt her thumb go through my belt loop, again, very delicately and softly although I knew she was a strong girl. And we danced. "Your own . . . personal . . . Jesus . . . ." We danced only briefly and she never said a word to me until we left the bar at midnight, then she asked me my name and we went home together.

I have never, since Nadia, reproduced the feelings of those last two weeks in America, nor gotten along so easily with another person, male or female. Everything was done easily; the undressing, the making of love, the mornings, the bathroom scenes, the good-byes, all were done with an art to them that I learned later is rare in this existence. Nadia added her worldview to everything, which was that of an artist intent on making life more beautiful, but with the intelligence to always do so easily and in a way that adds to the small incidents of life. She was, in fact, a careful person, and nothing like what she might seem from the outside, a sexy bartender in leather and jeans, although she was entirely that as well. We told one another everything the first night. She knew I would be there only two more weeks; she knew and entirely understood the whole CIA thing, and that it was my career.

Most of all though, she understood surfing.

Chapter Two

Technically, there is nothing that unique about surfing as a sport. It possesses an athletic portion, consisting of repeating a paddling motion arm by arm like a swimmer until the paddler reaches the "lineup," the starting point where the swell begins to break. It possesses a skill set that is developed and improved through experience, by riding many waves in a variety of circumstances. It possesses a thrill element consisting of gravity neutralization as the wave lifts the rider up, and the ride, which combines the above elements with the pleasant sensation of glide, along with pleasing sentiments of arc control. It also has a courage element that comes into play when circumstances become robust, as they frequently do in the surfing of larger waves. Fair enough?

Nonsense. This says nothing about surfing, the culture of surfing, and who surfs. Surfing is not a sport that can be broken down into its athletic elements. Surfing is a paradoxical juxtaposition of religion and sex, and surfers are not athletes, they are athletic radical bohemian poet-warrior buccaneers, traipsing everywhere, passionately in search of waves. They are high priests of smooth waters and early morning glass. They are musicians in the bowels of nature, pounding out their music on their digeredoos and calabash drums. They are lost tribes of animists, wild-eyed madmen. One must accept these truths in order to understand the culture of the sport; surfers are adventurers.

Nadia had plans as well. As I had imagined, Arlington, Virginia was not the last stop for her bus. She wanted to stay another few months and then head to Europe—Madrid she thought, to paint. What was so wonderful about our time together was the limits on both ends. That kind of thing happens. What is temporary by nature gives thoughts of permanence, but it is by its very impermanence that it exists. We would think of each other fondly and often, but we would not be together—that was how we phrased it—although there were moments when we really wanted to forget that separation was inevitable. I even considered staying longer in the States to develop this relationship further, but I knew I wouldn't, and that I would suffer as a result. But despite worry over the future and reminiscences, I thought mainly in the present, and for now it was wonderful.

We made the most of the last two weeks, which means of course, sex. From the first night after the bar until the scene at the airport, her bed was the place we would know one another, and in it we learned most of what we would remember. Nadia was compact and strong, and her body was the same olive color as her face. Were it not reddened with henna, her hair would be black, and so it was below. I remember the curves of her abdomen best and her light scent, which ran all about her, like a low-lying mist above a quiet sea.

Her body was of equal caliber to her mind and her talent; it was strong but not muscular, and she loved with a passion that often left her sobbing. At those times she would continue to cry in my arms until she calmed. I would never ask her about it, and she never would mention it, and I guess I was crying as well. That bed was our home in those two weeks and the home to our love, and we never sullied it by taking it on a bike ride or to the movies. It was not that we wouldn't have done those things, but there wasn't time, and that endowed our love with a quality I can only call urgency, and it meant, ultimately, sex. We experienced a spectrum of feelings together as our time came to an end. Finally, at Dulles Airport, our hands came apart and I walked down the jetway and boarded the airplane that would take me to Los Angeles and onward to Asia.

Three days later I arrived at Soekarno-Hatta Airport and came to a full stop. My layover in Hong Kong had been a blur of visiting a tailor and having suits made, and sleeping at the wrong times and shopping and beer. Now I sat on my bags in the terminal, taking in my first view of Indonesia. It was night and I was savoring the flavors of newness with a self-consciousness that was like holding a mirror up and watching yourself in it as you speak. The airport was a jungle and it was exciting to begin from zero, and to watch the brain try to cull them into some order as they took hold of me.

I knew nothing of this place. I had grown up in Rio de Janeiro and Lima and, before finishing high school in California, had traveled Latin America pretty extensively. I had surfed in Panama, Peru, Brazil and Mexico, none of which had anything to do with this. This was all part of the adventure and excitement I craved and was now beginning to register. My only uneasiness, and it was a big one, was that rather than getting to uncheck my boards and find a place to stay and scope out the surf, as on past adventures, my task was to meet my new boss, who would be picking me up at the airport, and to try to fit in with him. This was always difficult for me. I didn't really ever expect to have a boss, and each time it dawned on me that I had one, I was slightly surprised.

A tension had permeated everything that had led up to my arrival in Jakarta, in terms of my relationship with my new colleagues and the Station. Something was slightly off-kilter, and I couldn't put my finger on what it was. It occurred to me that Stokes had worked with these people for several years, and I wondered if he had issued some kind of general warning about me to them. That's what it felt like. I had been uneasy after my meeting with him, and I had received an odd cable from Jakarta Station asking exactly when I would be arriving, despite the fact that they already knew that. It was worded strangely, and I thought there was something behind it, some resistance to my coming.

The only people I knew from Jakarta Station were Stokes, who of course was gone now, and a crusty, old cold warrior, a Waspy type from the Vietnam era, what we call a real "Asia hand," who loitered around the Jakarta desk at Langley, talking about the old days in a wonderful colorful way, telling me how the fifth barstool at the Singapore Cricket Club had an imprint of his ass on it from so much time spent bellying up to the bar.

He was a great guy, but wouldn't be much help in this quagmire of Station politics. I had the gnawing feeling that Stokes had somehow poisoned the well. Or perhaps I had done it myself. I guess there's little worse you can say about a spy than "he's a surfer."

It was with these thoughts that I reached into my pouch and retrieved the shortened version of the cable containing my contact instructions. It was a much-folded slip of thermal paper that had been cut off at a tear-line from a longer cable containing alias names and other classified information. It instructed me to wait by the kiosk, outside of Customs, near the Garuda Indonesia counter. I found this easily enough and reviewing the paper again realized that my instructions assumed an arrival time of 2200 hours. Something was wrong, because I had arrived, and it was, by the clock on the wall (I had determined my mind wasn't up to deciphering how far ahead or behind my wristwatch was), 2000 hours, or exactly eight p.m.

I had no phone number to call, unless I wanted to try to reach someone at the embassy, like the Marine guard or somebody, and I didn't know where I was to live. In fact, I didn't, at that precise moment, know what in the hell I was doing there. I was to be met by my supervisor, my Branch Chief, one Mr. Larry Ridge, about whom I had heard nothing good. Even if he were on time, he wouldn't arrive for another two hours. This was not a good start for a new officer, and not a great show by the CIA in general.

I was full of energy, sort of. I was excited to be arriving, but exhausted from traveling, and very dazed and confused. My bags were off the plane, and I had brought a surf board with me as checked baggage. That should really impress my boss when he picked me up. Actually, I had several more boards coming, including two big wave guns, a longboard, a fun shape for smaller waves, and two more boards exactly like the one I brought on the plane. These were traveling boards, generally gunny shapes, designed for the power waves I would find in Indonesia, but not completely out of place on a smaller day either.

I got my bags together, put my board astride them and prepared to sit and read my guidebook while I waited. Surfers are always sitting around in airports, their unwieldy baggage consisting of one or two boards, backpacks and assorted brand name bags, waiting in some corner out of the traffic bouncing a hacky sack or reading a Lonely Planet guide or surf mag. Any one of them could be CIA, I suppose, because that is what I must have looked like that night.

Surfing the C.I.A.

The placement of the kiosk by the Garuda counter was unfortunate, in retrospect. Within minutes I had relaxed my principles and used *rupiah* someone had given me in Washington to purchase a frosty bottle of Bintang beer. It is amazing how dry they keep the atmosphere on those planes. It's a virtual desert. Soon the world began to look up and the details came more into focus in the well-lit airport.

To my palate, beer has a kind of wonderful soapy, eggy, round flavor that must be due to hops or something. The first big pull on a cold beer is special, like the first coffee in the morning, or the first smooth blue wave on a windless day. These things have the quality of newness and revelation, of virginity, and of course, deflorestation. They happen only once in that first-time way. What happens after the first beer goes down is influenced by that pleasant experience, and this frequently leads one to believe it can be recreated with another beer, which is what happened to me as I sat by the kiosk.

Time and thirst come to play a role in all of this as well, and can lead you to third and fourth beers; inebriation, of course, results from third and fourth beers, especially when those beers are liter-sized Bintangs with frost on their necks and you've been traveling for three days and are sitting on your luggage in a strange country late at night. That can lead you to forget completely about your new boss picking you up and you begin to think that all the world is your friend and there are not hostile forces out there working against you, especially among the Americans you have come to join.

A glow accompanies the experience of course, and is clearly visible to the outside viewer. There comes a point where only a thoroughly trained alcoholic can conceal what he has been doing for the past few hours. I was not such a seasoned drinker, so when Larry, the Branch Chief, arrived and discovered me, there was no concealing the fact that I was potted as a palm.

It was not exactly the start of a beautiful friendship. First of all, he wore too much cologne. I could smell that even through my beer and jet lag stench. The only remark he made to me on the ride was, "I thought you would be shorter." That told me something; I'm not sure what, but it wasn't good. Also, he looked right out of the Ralph Lauren catalogue: pink polo shirt, pressed designer jeans, dock shoes—a very natty gringo with not a hair out of place. He looked like a college tennis coach who was retaining his physique at some effort, the kind of coach who wouldn't give independent study credit for surfing.

That ride from the airport to Kebayoran was among the least comfortable of my life. I was fascinated by what went by outside, and exhausted and exhilarated, and, of course, drunk. I wanted to run out and feel it all, smell it all, taste it all. I was exalted by my arrival, by my own existence, but I was also pretty spaced out, thinking three and five things at once. I wanted to tell him I was happy to be here and that this was all super fucking fascinating to me, you know, that lady with the wrap on her head, those guys with the sarongs walking in the traffic. These were real topics. I sank back into silence as the car moved into the well-lit area along Jalan Sudirman.

The Hilton appeared on the right and then receded as we rounded a traffic circle and glided into a neighborhood. In there, all was calm. Large trees hung over the road, and the houses were massive, white Dutch constructions on lots surrounded by high walls and trees. Each house had a man stationed outside, some in small guard shacks in front of large driveway porticos. Some wore uniforms, others wore uniforms and batik head scarves and sarongs. Some talked together in groups of two or three. Heavy black cars sat in front of a block-long wall, parked half on the grass. Here and there a vendor pushed a stall.

We slid into a driveway at the end of a small road and a diminutive figure ran to open the gate. He smiled as we entered, holding the gate open; a short white dog jumped around him. This was Parto, the houseboy, guard, butler, gardener, mechanic, sometime chauffeur, and valet. His wife was the cook, it was explained. The dog, short-legged and grinning like the man, leaped and yelped with glee. Larry and I had given up trying to communicate. I apologized for being so tired, but he knew I was kind of smashed anyway. I thanked him and said goodnight.

I fell asleep, but woke after a while in that old Dutch house, the air conditioner turned up to arctic, a silken hum pouring a stream of twentieth-century cool over me. The house was stucco, with large round holes in every wall, which I guess were used to ventilate. This house was classic Asia colonial with a heavy, solid feel, and cool in the tropical night. It was about half furnished by the embassy, with a sofa, beds, chairs and tables. Although the air was on, the ceiling fan was turning. The floor was red tile, very cool to my bare feet.

I wondered at being awake, and then I heard what had roused me. It was the call to prayer from a speaker on top of a mosque some streets over. How weird and exotic and right-on. It was dark and cool and I was alone in that old Dutch house, standing there in my boxers, with that new weird sound. It's no mistake being here, I thought. Whatever the cost, whatever must be endured, it is right that I am here. That is what I was thinking, in the early hours of morning, on my first night in Java, as I listened in the darkness to those minor tones chanted out into the night . . . the discordant minor chords of Islam.

In my dream, I came to Indonesia from Peru, as some kind of surfing ambassador. It was my job to officially promote surfing in Peru, and I couldn't stop talking about Peru and the waves there. I went through all the long-anticipated introductions at the embassy, which would be happening for real the next day. I dreamed I was telling the Marine at the embassy that the transition from Peru to Indonesia was a radical one, although much less heavy on my head than a return to the States would have been. Then I was telling a Consular Officer about my adjustment. I said mainly I had to adjust to faster waves, stronger dope and no weird dickhead Maoists blowing stuff up all the time. I told the Political Counselor and the Deputy Chief of Mission that I had surfed some pretty big waves in Peru; I was ready with a couple of boards that would work in the Indian Ocean, and of course I had been staring at photos of Uluwatu, G-Land and Lagundi for years in the surf magazines. I explained formally to the ambassador that I was a soul surfer, globe-hopping and working to pay the bills, nothing more. I explained that I was the only diplomatic surfer around, and if they fired me at any time I would shine the trip home and stay right where I was. The ambassador listened politely as I told him I knew that out here most of the CIA guys had families, some bitch making them miserable, or some kid who would get more expensive over the years, or some mortgaged house in Reston, Virginia or someplace enslaving them. He nodded and said, "Right on, Dude."

I was saying all this in my dream when a horn sounded outside. It was Monday, my first day of work. The embassy shuttle left without me.

My taxi got me to work two hours late. You get a certain amount of latitude, however, when you're brand new, especially if you're on your first tour. There is an assumption that you don't know how to put your pants on. The assumption goes beyond thinking you are inexperienced in the art of espionage. The assumption is that you are a total moron. I guess they had it about right.

Chapter Three

I got a break early in my tour, like the second week. Since I was so green and in need of some seasoning, they sent me as far from the Station as I could get, to screw up there. When I got called to the Station Chief's office, I thought I was going to get my ass chewed, but instead I got this great deal. I would go to North Sumatra to meet this agent who was passing through since there was nobody up there to meet him. The guy was a businessman from Kuala Lumpur who had interests up in Aceh, where Westerners were not allowed to travel due to the Islamic fundamentalists who were trying to split from Indonesia.

North Sumatra is not only a radical spot for fundamentalist Muslims and a separatist movement that drove Suharto crazy, it also has about the best freaking right point break on just about the entire planet. So I would be hitting exotic Lagundi Bay in Pulau Nias. I couldn't believe it. Of course, I had all of Indo mapped out as to where the best surf was, but

Surfing the C.I.A.

I couldn't believe I would be getting my first dose of surf in one of the hottest waves in the world. I couldn't get packed fast enough.

Nobody in the Station wanted to go to North Sumatra. For them, there was no reason. The agent I would be meeting was unimportant and there was little chance of meeting anyone else up there because Medan, the capital of Sumatra, was just a merchant town with the usual rank-and-file schlock bureaucrats and semi-military officialdom, which is a universal and ubiquitous force in Indonesia, hanging around picking up protection money from the Chinese merchants. I knew they were sending me up there because nobody else wanted to go.

The radical Muslin scene in Aceh province, at the northernmost end of Sumatra, was also a disincentive. The area was under a semipermanent travel advisory due to violence between the Indonesian troops and the villagers, who frequently got strafed from helicopters and fought back with rocks. (I think some Indo generals had seen too many Vietnam movies.)

So I packed—no suit, just some street clothes—some writing stuff, a book by Henry Miller and my seven foot thruster tri-fin big wave board.

The flight up was uneventful, and I got in to Medan just in time for the meeting on Thursday afternoon. My plan was to get everything done Thursday, but act like I had to meet the guy again on Friday, then stay through the weekend and surf and travel home Monday, unless it was sick good, like six to eight foot, whereupon another agent meeting might have to be set.

I had my super clandestine, double-secret-handshake commo (communication) plan, which was simply to call the guy up and say that I was Mr. Case, and could he come and meet me at the usual place. Not real fucking spooky, but I was nervous enough anyway. I thought I should have been more nervous going to my first meeting with a recruited agent, but this guy was a businessman, which gave him a good cover for a meeting with a U.S. Embassy official if we were spotted or anyone asked him about it later. Anyway, it just didn't seem very clandestine, which it wasn't. They never would have sent me if it were anything important. Nonetheless, I went through my Surveillance Detection Route, made my stops just as we had done in training, and tried to act CIA-like.

"The usual place" turned out to be the best Chinese restaurant of my life—a hole in the wall even for this rabbit warren city, impossible to find, but worth coming halfway round the world for. It featured *mei tsai kou rou*, a pork roast that tasted like it was soaked in cannabis and was totally addictive.

The agent had nothing to say.

"Still radical up in Aceh?" I asked.

"Yeah."

"Okay," I said, "I will report that." I took a bunch of notes and decided to save them for my first day back to the office where I could waste a day writing up an elaborate report, rather than try to organize them now and waste precious play time. "Try to remain available tomorrow," I told him, "and even

Monday, because that sounds interesting and I will be standing by in case Washington wants to know more." I also instructed him very formally that this restaurant would be our usual meeting place until further notice, which is no doubt what my predecessor Case Officer had had the good sense to do as well. I made a note to check on who that Officer was and look him up sometime. This agent was met infrequently, but there was an increasing interest from Headquarters about Muslim stuff, which is why I was here. The situation with this agent was pretty clearly that we pretended to be interested in what he told us, and he pretended to have something interesting to say.

I went back to the hotel and found out the next plane for Nias would be early Friday. I had plenty of time to hit the town.

In the lobby, I asked the Concierge about night life. A large, boyish-looking Chinese guy was standing there—he looked safe enough, not gay or anything—and chimed in in half-ass English that he would be glad to show me around. I went for it, and soon we were driving around Medan in his Mercedes Baby Benz, as he called it.

He told me his name was Sam, which seemed as likely as anything else. I gave him the old cover story, that I was just a tourist but also looking to do business, as most Americans in Southeast Asia do. He said good, and took me to his bar, and I do mean *his* bar. He owned this place that was half disco whorehouse and half Egyptian spa. It was the weirdest looking deal, with lights and a dance floor, then a tiled walkway that led to a gymnasium and steam rooms, all with Ra and Tutankamen decor. It was still early, and it was obvious that he did not want to hang out here, but just brought me by to show me his harem, which consisted of about thirty Indonesian whores who were particularly ugly and surly as a group, lolling about waiting for the trade to come in.

We went to a little hotel bar nearby. The place was packed with Chinese and Indonesian business types and hookers. At some point three *bulehs* appeared in the bar, two of whom were typically drunk Aussies grabbing the girls and nearly falling off their bar stools. The third guy wasn't drunk, and he wasn't interested in the whores. He said he would hold out and look for some real women, at which everyone laughed. Had I known him better at the time, I would have put money on him scoring that night with a supermodel from Paris. He was not overly big, nor did he look like a weight trainer or anything. He was standing there at the bar in a loose T-shirt and cut-off jeans, sandals and a pony tail. He looked to me like any typical tourist hippie type traveling through Asia and hanging out.

The women in the bar noticed him, and after a few made overtures and were rebuffed, you could see that they were making nasty remarks about him. Nonetheless, from time to time he would smile at one of them, and she would slink over straight away, only to be sent off again without so much as a slap on the ass.

He told me his name was Ailbhis Finn. "Call me Elvis, like your American man Presley," he said. He said he'd sailed over from Singapore with some pirates on the Java Sea. That sounded exaggerated, although plausible, but I didn't know Elvis then. More likely he left out the sensational parts. He gave me a number in Singapore. "Come up there next month. Beers will be my shout." Elvis was Irish all right.

I asked him what he had been doing before this trip through Asia. He said he just got out of the Army. This turned out to be the French Army, Paratroops. "I just got discharged from the French Foreign Legion. I did service in Chad and Djibouti, and then I was made a trainer of the mountain brigade in the hills of Corsica. That kept me rather fit." He had a deep Irish laugh and he used it on himself with no mercy. I thought he was either a really cool guy or totally full of shit. He reminded me to contact him in Singapore next month when he got back . . . "his shout."

Elvis vowed to find a real woman; I told him I had not come ten thousand miles to screw a tourist, if that is what he meant. Hoo Haw, he laughed. I looked at this guy, a picture of vitality. He was more or less blond, deeply tan, with a ponytail pulled back from a tough, handsome face. An old scar crossed his left eye, but apparently had left the eye undamaged. "I don't go for these tarts, Cunty," he said, addressing me with my new name.

I liked the guy, and I wanted to talk more, but I was nervous about my cover story, and I was thinking suspiciously, still being pretty new at all of this. After all, I really didn't know what I was doing yet. I was pretty green, and I knew it, not just about the job, but about Asia. It's a big continent that

I knew almost nothing about, and I was alone in Sumatra talking to a dangerous-looking Irish cowboy, who could be IRA for all I knew, and who would not be appearing in my trip report. This guy was cool though, so impulsively I took him aside, probably too dramatically, and gave him my business card, the first one I had ever handed out. It read:

Guthrie M. Hayes
Second Secretary, Political Section
Embassy of the United States of America
Jakarta, Indonesia

"Good on you Cunty, U.S.A. Embassy, yeah? Do you know the Marines?" I told him I knew them, though I barely did. He said, "I have been dating the Woman Marine from the embassy in Singapore. Why not come up for the Marines' birthday next month? You got to be there, Cunt."

That was all he said. I looked out the door and watched this nutcase jog away into the Sumatra night, thinking how strange the conversation had been. In the end, it was the most normal event of the evening.

The two Aussies from the bar were too drunk to be interesting anymore, so I was left alone with Sam. Next thing you know, we were back in the Baby Benz, cruising Medan, North Sumatra. The first stop was like a cartoon. It billed itself as a striptease place, but the poor thing finished her act in her panty hose, with a finale consisting of her taking off her bra. When she did that, the lights in the place went out. It was an absurdly prudish strip act, and she had rolled around so much on the wooden stage that she had dust all over her stockings.

We had a few beers there and concluded that this was not going to be a hot spot for genuine sleaze. I was hungry for some conversation, or at least a look at the sexual provender here in Sumatra. It seemed a shame to be here and not experiment.

By midnight, we found ourselves in another bar with an atmosphere a little less pathetic. I sat at the bar watching the girls dancing suggestively with each other, demonstrating the same restraint of that striptease act. This appeared to be an Indonesian thing, maybe a Muslim take on the Thai presentation, which is much more direct and overt. The whole thing was weird and funny from one perspective, but provocative and sensual from the other.

I looked around the bar. There were some Japanese at a table, a lone German, and various groups of Sino-Indonesians, probably local business types. The place was tiresome, and Sam was clearly planning to show off his own club, so we went back to the King Tut place.

"You and you frens my guess!" he said.

"What?" I asked.

"You drik free. Wanna wiskee?"

"Beer. Sam, I speak some Indonesian," I said, and Sam and I drank for free. I wondered if there was a catch, but there didn't seem to be one. Actually there would be, but it was so weird that it wouldn't even qualify as a catch in my normal understanding of that term. Sam was not satisfied with his show of hospitality. He chatted with me politely for a while but the whole time I was waiting for the other shoe to hit me.

Finally, he turned to me and said, "You wan fuck girl?" Clearly Sam was not just the owner of the bar but also of the girls. I surveyed the thirty or so whores distributed around the place trying to size up a candidate. "No no," said Sam. "No these girl. My accountant. These girl Indonesia. Accountant China. Free. You Fuck Free." I thought it over and agreed to fuck his accountant. It was a pretty easy decision, and I had no idea what it meant. It could have been a hypothetical question for all I knew, and on the other hand some old bat wearing nothing but a green eyeshade might appear. I was now somewhat drunk, fortunately for all concerned.

Sam took me upstairs and led me into a dim room with a bed, then disappeared. I was reminded of a visit to a doctor's office. The nurse leads you into the exam room and you sit there thinking about stealing all of the stuff in the medical cabinet while you wait for the doctor. Sam returned after ten minutes and knocked on the door. "She coming."

"Already?" I asked, drunkenly, laughing at my joke. He just grinned dumbly. Sam then turned out the light and took a seat. I had not even noticed there was a chair there. I lay back on the bed and said nothing. After a few more minutes someone, a woman, spoke in a Chinese dialect at the door. Sam got up and let her in. Strangely, he again took his seat in the corner. The girl came over to the bed and began to undress. I just stared at her in the darkness. She noticed my inactivity of course, and said something in Chinese to Sam.

"You take off close," he told me. "She want you take off close."

"Sam," I said, "don't you have customers downstairs?"

"Ha ha," said Sam, "I stay or she afraid. You eat her pussy, okay?"

"Sam," I said, "Sam . . . ." I was really at a loss for words. I was kind of drunk, she was kind of attractive, although I never did see her in the light. When we were finished, Sam let himself and the accountant out of the room.

I got dressed quickly and went down to the bar, where I tried to make some sense of the evening. The worst part about it was that she talked to Sam the whole time. I had gotten him to turn his chair toward the wall, but by no means would he leave the room. She enjoyed herself, but she was communicating with two men the whole time, albeit via different media, one verbally, the other sexually, and it was clearly her lay, her conquest, not mine. All in all, it was a bit strange, but I had an early call to surf.

The prop plane touched down on the dirt runway. The wind sock by the field hung down like a flaccid condom. I was in severe hangover shock, and the strange night's events stuck to me like a scent. I had packed my street clothes in the bottom of my rucksack and was now my surfer self, traveling in shorts and sandals and feeling like anything but a bureaucrat, nothing less than CIA, and happy despite the slow withdrawal of the alcohol. I had hooked up with a Japanese surfer, who, aside from the fact that he could only read English and not speak it, was pretty cool. His shiny black hair fell halfway down his back. Once we landed, and while I was getting coffee and waiting for the jeep to take us to the surf, he slipped away and had his head shaved. I meant to ask him what was up with that, but never got around to it.

The jeep ride to Lagundi Bay took over two hours, during which I was quite certain I would die. It was hotter than fuck and we were seated sideways in the back of an old Land Cruiser with no shocks. We finally got there after a trip through jungle and riverbeds, which must be impassable at some times of the year.

Pulau Nias is famous for its warrior history. They have these shows where the guy gets up in full primitive armor and runs thirty yards straight at a stone wall and then jumps over it, presumably to the surprise of the defenders on the other side. It's a cool show, but I guess it wasn't real effective as a combat tactic, because there doesn't seem to be any conquered land acquired that way. I guess higher walls stopped them.

We had a couple shots of the ocean from the jeep, which seemed to be driving down the center of the island. I was recovering and beginning to take increased interest in the coastline. My board was in a good board bag on the roof of the jeep, and the Nip and I were the only surfers from the plane. The rest were German nudists, who are usually the second set of pioneers to hit a place after surfers discover it.

Finally, I knew we were getting close. There is something about a surf spot; you just know when you are near one, especially in the Third World. It seems like something intangible, but maybe not. Maybe you see a few native kids wearing surf trunks, castoff Katins or Quicksilvers; maybe you see haircuts that look familiar, or you smell surfboard wax. Who knows, but I believe I could wake up in one of those places, whether in Tahiti or France or Brazil or wherever, and discern a note in the air that is absent in the rest of that country. I felt it strongly in Pulau Nias. It felt suddenly like Hawaii rather than an island off the coast of Sumatra. Then I heard it and a chill went down my back. I heard the unmistakable thunder of surf.

Lagundi is a bay on the west side of this island off the coast of North Sumatra, where the palms swing out over the water before they grow upward. The waves are legend among surfers, who first discovered the place a few years back. I can imagine the first guy to arrive with a board. Probably there were a few nude Germans not far behind him. There was, no doubt, lots of malaria and a few huts where he bought *nasi-goreng*, a typically Indonesian rice dish—and that's about it. (I was on doxycyclene pills to prevent malaria. Word had it an Aussie had died here from getting malaria under his skull.)

This place was just a *desa*, a village, where fishermen could predict danger from the sea based on the precise shape of the waves coming into the bay and their consistent form. The wave is absolutely perfect, breaking down the beach with an edge like a machete, breaking over a reef that runs along the side of the bay, the reef following the shoreline and making the waves break in a repetitive almost monotonously consistent right tube. The backdrop of green palm trees finished off the paradise feeling, and if you paid for a meal they gave you a place to sleep for free.

Nicholas Ware

I was a little edgy taking off on my first wave. I always feel a little funny in a new place. Add to it the fact that I am ten thousand miles from my local break and still not entirely sure how I got here, hungover and somewhat in shock from having had weird sex with a stranger while she talked to someone else, and assorted other aspects of cultural bombardment with which I had been shelled; I was really doing okay considering.

I had never set foot in the Indian Ocean before, and the waves looked very powerful. I took my time and looked down through the clear, blue crystal as I paddled toward the lineup. A few guys were out, but a lot of waves were coming through unridden. I chose a medium-size wave and spun around, launching my board with a thrust. I dropped in and turned, being far too conservative, and I was way out on the shoulder and out of the impact zone before I knew it. Nonetheless, the wave caught up with me, breaking perfectly with no sections, and gave me plenty of time to play with the hook. I probably looked like a kook from the beach, but then nobody was on the beach except some old ladies and what looked like some Australian girls getting sun on their breasts. Anyway, I didn't care; I didn't have the place wired yet. Shit, I was still getting used to being wet again.

My next wave rose before me. This time I drove straight down into the bowl and threw my tail against the flat water in front of the wave. I put both hands into the face and felt it lift me up, board and all. I felt suddenly weightless, and I thought I was going to go over the falls for sure, but instead I just hung there, not falling, not accelerating, just there, right in the tube, weightless, with only foam and spray seeming to hold me against the face of the wave. Then I landed and was able to drive the board way out into the blue water and over the back of the wave. No wave, no other wave in the world, had ever treated me that well. I surfed until the late afternoon.

The Nip was out there too, and we came in and made insane faces at one another and maniacal gestures trying to communicate all of this. He only understood English on paper, but screw writing things down, I wanted to scream it.

I decided his name was Sanyo. He was very agreeable, and we cruised up the beach with a beer and tried to talk. There were still some guys out surfing, and it looked like an evening session in California, except for the massive palm trees framing the scene of perfect six- to eight-foot point break surf with waves going by empty. That does not happen in California.

We found a decent *losmen*, a homestay lodging, with a ping-pong table below it. The *losmens* were spread all along the point. Each one had a house, built of wood and palm frond mats, with steps up or a ladder, a sleeping room upstairs and a separate house for the owner's family. Our *losmen*, which we called Superman's, had the only ping-pong table. We had a few beers and played some ping-pong, and then Sanyo did a wonderful thing: even though he spoke no English, he wrote it, and apparently penning a mean hand, he managed to pick up the Australian girls.

Chapter Four

I returned to Jakarta, and on Monday night I actually got some sleep, back in the old Dutch house with the AC all the way up. When the embassy vanpool, the Batmobile, showed up in the morning, I boarded and even had a nice word for the dotty embassy secretaries, the old bats that gave the vehicle its name.

Those waves had been epic. The feeling would get me through at least until Wednesday. Krebs and Farley, the two second-tour officers at the embassy, upperclassmen of the Station, were their usual disgusting sycophantic selves, but in fairness I guess they were just as high from golf and church as I was from what I had been doing. Actually, that's pure bullshit. No one in that embassy was as high as me. I couldn't wait to set up another surf trip.

I was still the new guy, but now I was the tan, recently laid new guy (Sanyo and I scored with the Aussie girls), and at least I was beginning to enjoy myself outside of the embassy.

Surfing the C.I.A.

Still, the embassy and all the CIA stuff, especially the rules, were increasingly a reminder of high school. The Station was made up of jocks, and I was the stoner/surfer on the fringes. They were all married as well, and even when they tried to be nice they just ended up having me over to sit around their living room. I just wasn't down with that and wanted to head directly to the bars and have a beer and talk to the whores.

I probably had more in common with the whores than with the standard suburban Americans who were the embassy population. The embassy people kind of accepted me, but underneath I think they thought I was pretty weird and possibly dangerous, at least to the preservation of their values. I was continually confused though, as I had lived overseas a lot of my life, and to me this was not a foreign country in the same way as for them. California was home, true, but Indonesia could become home easily. All I would need is a nice chick and I would be laughing.

I also had Station politics to contend with. Someone's stock was always rising or falling. Krebs and Farley were the frontrunners all the time, but sometimes one was ahead of the other, depending on what was hot at the moment. Headquarters was sending out these cryptic (I guess that was normal) messages about Islamic activity, and we all knew that Iraq was about to make some kind of move. Saddam Hussein was a dick, that was pretty clear, although I never really understood what side he was on relative to the Iranians, or what was really going on in the Middle East, or in the world in general, which can't be a good sign for a spy.

Anyway, Krebs was on to something, and it was being kept pretty closed up. He was gone all morning in the Front Office, and, although he kept it quiet all day, I could tell he was pleased with himself. I had a feeling he was making progress with some Muslim stuff. Farley's demeanor confirmed it. Although they were buddies and normally very thick together, it was clear that Krebs was now firmly in the lead. "When do the 13s come out?" I asked Farley. I knew he was hoping to get promoted and would be humiliated if Krebs made GS-13 this time and he didn't. I was a GS-9.

That night I went down to The Sportsman Grill in Blok M. I had been down in that area before, but after Sumatra I was ready to really check out the Jakarta bar scene, and Blok M was the main event. Also, it was close to my house, and now that I was beginning to get my bearings, I could get to and from there in a *becak* or a *bajai*. *Becaks* were more fun because you could ride silently in the pedicab while the driver pedaled, but *bajais* were quicker, with their motorbike engines and three-wheeled maneuverability.

The little street, Jalan Pelatehan, was lined with bars, most of which seemed under construction of some kind. The Sportsman Grill was the most respectable of them evidenced by the presence of Western women sitting with oil guys at tables and at the bar. It was modeled after a sports bar in the States and had satellite shows from the States and videos of rugby and soccer. After a couple of beers, I got brave and decided to check out the other bars on the street.

The next one down was called Betty's Place. I walked in and immediately recognized a Turkish diplomat I'd met once at the embassy. He was holding a pool cue in one hand and a beer in the other. He looked mesmerized, and I could see the reason. For the next four hours, we watched the amazing Snake Woman play pool. She was radical. First of all, she had about the greatest ass in Java. Her legs, long and shapely, had the sprayed-on jeans look going. So that was one part of her act, the back.

But what was happening in front was the business. Aside from the fact that you could see her breasts, which, by the way, you could also see from a certain angle behind her, she was really a talented pool player. She beat three oil workers while we watched. Most of the time, for simple shots, she held the cue in one hand, perfectly steady, and would shoot combinations and everything like that. I am pretty ignorant of the actual logistics of billiards, but that Chinese whore playing pool was a show.

The Snake Woman wasn't entirely Chinese. Her father was from Sumatra somewhere, but she had that exotic look in her features that spoke of origins in the north of Asia. Her nose looked like it had been broken, but it fit in somehow with her face and gave her sultry look—a kind of sympathetic appeal. She had a space between her teeth, and her long black hair made her look pretty, if a little sleazy and rough. I mean, she was still a whore and all. She was tall for a girl in the bars, her body was well proportioned, and she was strong. Jesus was she strong.

Aside from a great ass and a sexy overall persona, she possessed a star quality. Under other circumstances, Snake Woman would have been on stage, but Indonesia does not have the Patpong scene found in Thailand, with strip shows and sex acts, as my Sumatra trip had demonstrated.

It was easy to see how you could fall in love with one of these girls. In fact, someone had fallen in love with the Snake Woman. Some guy had married her two years before and taken her to London. She stayed a month then hauled ass back to the bars in Jakarta, acting tough as ever, although I reckon it took its toll. She said her father was a Kung-Fu teacher for the Indonesian Army. I never knew if that was true or not. We asked her why they called her Snake Woman. Her real name was Florida. "It's because I lie," she said.

Once my fascination with Snake Woman subsided, I realized that I had made an important contact. This Turk, Kamal Atta, was number two in his embassy. He was an arrogant fuck and really spoke his mind. His build was hefty, overweight, but obviously strong. He had a large head of hair, very curly, almost like an afro, and wore thick glasses. I asked him if he knew anyone from the U.S. Embassy, half expecting him to tell me he played golf with Krebs. He told me "hell no," that he did not fool around with diplomats, but spent his time travelling and screwing the girls. He had been in Indonesia nearly a year and estimated he had copulated more than three hundred women. That was better than London, where in the same time period he estimated only one hundred English girls and seventy-five of other nationalities, mostly Japanese tourists.

"Those girls would show up in Picadilly swinging their underpants over their heads," he marveled.

He said he liked the United States, but that New York had been a big disappointment. He had expected Americans to be taller and blonde; instead, he was met with an assortment of swarthy immigrants. "I can find that in Europe!" The place he wanted to see was California. There you had blondes, sunshine, good music, fast cars.

"Ever been surfing?" I asked him.

"No, but that sounds good."

"Bitchin," I said.

Eventually, we moved to another bar, then another. Finally, we found ourselves in a place called the Tambora, which was, from the looks of it, the late night wind-up spot. Snake Woman was there. She had disappeared from Betty's Place, and we assumed she had gone home with some oil guy, but she reappeared as though out of smoke and was watching herself dance in the mirror. She looked like she was stoned out of her mind; I figured it was Ecstasy.

The bar was between two rooms, one with music, one without. The crowd was tightly packed into the music room where hard disco and flashing lights gave the place an eerie, dark coldness. The other room provided relief from the music. The girls were in both places, but the crowd was very mixed. It was a sweaty, jolly and very intense place, full of whores and gangster-looking men, the seamy underbelly of Southeast Asia. A very good bar. The Snake Woman was dancing by herself against the mirror in the music room. She was grinding and thrusting provocatively. As I watched her, a *buleh* guy came up and put his hands on her waist. She let him go on awhile, and then abruptly stopped dancing and jerked away from him. She gave him the finger, and then she looked at him and stuck her finger in her mouth before turning away. The guy just shook his head.

Kamal and I wandered from one room to the other. He was pretty tanked by this time, as was I. For the first time in my tour, I had a conversation about world events. He gave me his perspective on the Middle East. He said that Turkey had some traditional enemies and was in favor of moderate Islam, which was practiced in the traditions established by Kamal Ataturk, his namesake. This was relevant to Indonesia, which was the largest Muslim nation, yes, but as they were of the Sunni tradition, it was not the same Islam. He predicted that war would break out, as it was clear that Saddam Hussein had designs on the oil fields of Kuwait. The Iraqis, he said, from the Indonesian perspective, were closer to them in faith.

He talked great. He punctuated everything with emotional emphasis, calling everyone bastards and thieves. "You watch, that bastard thief will annex Kuwait. You American bastards should not sit by and watch this." He spoke with a British accent, and informed me he had been educated at the Sorbonne and was fluent in French, as well.

The guy rejected guy by Snake Woman, aka Florida, came over to the bar. "Nice try," I said.

"She'll never go with me, I'm too poor," he said. The guy was Australian, and did look a little down on his luck.

Surfing the C.I.A.

He told me his name was Stretch, "or that's what my mates call me. I reckon it's my name." The guy proceeded to tell me and Kamal his story. He was a cowboy, a Jackaroo, from the northern part of Australia. He had worked for ten years on a sheep station, then had come to Indonesia on his way to Nepal. He'd been in Jakarta just over a year, and was looking to get into some kind of business, but so far he had only landed a job working for the Jakarta sanitation company, driving a garbage truck. Kamal laughed so hard he nearly had a coughing fit.

"Reckon I smell like rubbish," Stretch said. "No wonder Florida gives me the brush-off." I had read about the Jakarta dumps in *Twilight in Jakarta*, by Mochtar Lubis. I could only imagine the stench of the place.

"Hey, Florida, here's a man for you, an American," said Stretch. She had just appeared at the bar.

"I know him. He's my boyfriend. Hi boyfriend." Snake Woman gave my arm a squeeze. Stretch laughed.

"You should take her home," Kamal said, "Just look at her ass."

Snake Woman scowled at him, then shook her ass good-naturedly. "This all I got," she said.

What happened after that was difficult to remember. I woke up with Snake Woman in my bed. Stretch and somebody were in the guest room. I mechanically got up and showered, and even made the Batmobile. Before I left, I nudged Snake Woman and asked her if she wanted some money. She hugged the pillow and misquoted Dire Straits: "Money for nothing, sex for free." I left them all in the house for Parto and his wife to worry about. Stretch practically lived there in the guest room from then on.

At the embassy staff meeting, we learned that Saddam Hussein had invaded Kuwait.

Chapter Five

Something else changed after my Sumatra trip. I was no longer a cherry. I had lost my CIA virginity by meeting that inconsequential agent up there, whom I never got back to because I was too busy surfing with Sanyo and speaking Australian. It was a non-meeting by all standards, but it was my first one and it was out of the way. I was now two months into my tour and they would either have to give me my accounts or send me home. I had done nothing substantive for the U.S. government in the two years since I joined the Agency and went into training. Amazing how much money they would spend.

I was right. During the next two weeks, the Station gave me three more inconsequential agents to handle. The first meetings with these guys I would not handle alone. Another officer would be present and make the turn-over to me. So off we went to meet Genius/1, a mid-level political strategist for the ruling Indonesian party, Golkar.

Genius/1, or G/1 for short, had been reporting to the Agency for fifteen years. His reporting was accurate, predictable, and totally ignored. He was supplementing his income without doing any physical labor and had little reason for concern. I couldn't see why they kept him on, but I was nervous because this time I would be chaperoned and my colleagues would be scrutinizing my handling of the situation, which would probably cause me to fuck it up even more than normal.

Back in the office, I wrote up the meeting:

```
TO: Headquarters INFO Singapore, Kuala
    Lumpur, Bangkok

CODEWORD MARS TOPSIDE LUCKY MICHAEL

SUBJECT: Meeting GENIUS/1 turnover to
         GABRIEL M. SNOOK intel report
         to follow.
```

1. On this date, GENIUS/1 (G/1) was turned over to new Case Officer SNOOK by Wilfred O. ADAIR. Meeting was conducted in location 13 after two hour Surveillance Detection Route (SDR) which revealed no surveillance.
2. G/1 accepted turnover and was in good spirits. Snook was able to build rapport and extract intel report (I27454) which is being submitted separately. G/1 reported that his niece is now living in USA and that he will be visiting her following the Moslem fasting month of Ramadan. Station requests arrangements be made to re-polygraph G/1 at that time

```
and G/1 requests he receive a physical
examination for blood pressure at that
time as well. As Headquarters will re-
call, G/1 has received this service from
U.S. doctors annually in the past and it
has boded well for his reporting and mo-
rale, and serves in lieu of an annual
cash bonus.
3. G/1 reports that he met with a member of
the main opposition movement recently and
believes this individual (identity pro-
vided separately) may be a future source
of intelligence.
4. Next meeting is set for 15 December,
location 09 at 1900 hours.
```

Having written my first cable from one of my own cases, I decided it would be good to establish a similar pattern of surf-reporting to my home-bro back in California, Dale Sweeney, who was living in Santa Barbara, surfing a lot and working as a waiter at the Charthouse to meet girls. Sweeney was a trip. He would never have to worry about money, so he just did cool experimental things with every imaginable kind of water and land vehicle, made surfing films, and did other waterman/trust-fund activities. So I wrote:

```
SWEENEY TODD PRICK DICK ASSWIPE SUPER
SECRET SURF SOMETHING
Imagine if you will:

   Your life has sucked for the last three
hours. You have been sweating in an aluminum
can with four-wheel drive as it pounds your
ass through gully and rut to a point stick-
ing out in the Indian Ocean which holds the
promise, and the roar of surf. You walk to
```

```
the beach in a dreamlike state, eyes closed,
feeling the goodness of warm sand under-
foot.
   You open your eyes. You think you are
still in bed because all you see is your big
blue, corduroy quilt. As you focus you think
you see some bedbugs or fleas or something
crawling around on the blue corduroy quilt.
There are not many fleas, only four or five,
and they are climbing and dropping on the
blue corduroy.
   The blue corduroy now comes into focus as
the Indian Ocean. Your view is partially
obstructed by a large white image on your
screen, partially blocking out the sea. In
your lens eye view you focus on the obstacle
in the foreground and find it to be a D-cup
Australian breast.
   A flash of color obstructs your vision
and suddenly you appear to be in a field of
flowers, which you redefine as her bikini
bottoms. It is still her. Then this woman
smiles and your fish-eye lens goes white in
a snowstorm of ivory.
   You fall down.

   Enclosed are photos of Nias and girlflesh
to prove what I say is true.

Locked in, Gus.
```

There was a lot of hustle and bustle in the Station and, as usual, I was out of it. I was beginning to wise up to the fact that the skill set of a good Case Officer included the ability to become an insider, not just with the host country government, but also with Station management, and that the most important recruitment was not of an intelligence source, but of the person who would write your evaluation. In other words, it appeared as though the energy that should be aimed at the enemy was aimed at climbing the ladder. This was not surprising really, I just wasn't very good at it. I never got the swing of kissing ass without appearing to be kissing ass. It was being practiced in the Station though, as high art.

Krebs, Farley, and Larry Ridge were more cliquish than ever. They were now rejoicing over winning the softball league finals. I could see how well Stokes must have fit in with this group.

Jack Rosen, known as JR, was back from his home leave in the States, and I got my first chance to talk to him. Even before he left he had seemed to be different from the rest of the Station officers—quieter, smarter. He was also working on something separate and seemed to spend a lot of time out of the office. When he came in, he would write at his computer for a while, and be gone again. He sat at his desk and covered his work with his body, so you might never get a glimpse of what he was writing or reading. He was coming into focus as a totally different kind of officer from Farley and Krebs. He did not appear to have any interest in talking, joining golf clubs, or any of the normal, hail-fellow-well-met IBM salesman crap procedures. The rest of the officers treated him with a mixture of distance and respect.

He listened carefully as I asked him some initial questions about how things worked. I didn't get much out of him, but it was clear that he understood what I was saying. I was getting anxious to get his take on things and I pressed, asking him what he thought about the group here and the mission of this

Station. He cut me off. "Make haste slowly," was all he would say. Later on, I noticed he had dropped a brochure for a skin diving tour on my desk.

My plan for the weekend was to fly to Singapore to attend the Marine Corps Birthday Ball. I was invited by Sally, a friend from Washington with whom I had had a flirtation the previous year. She was now serving as a Visa Officer in Singapore. Since she was not CIA, she was having a totally different experience in Southeast Asia than I was.

Singapore looks like a big shopping mall with tidy people crawling all over it and everything clean. The motorcycles are big compared to the tiny ones in Java, and prosperous Chinese steward everything along. Coming out of Jakarta, it's like a big breath of fresh air and clean water. You can open your mouth in the shower.

Parts of Singapore still held the old charm despite the frantic development and destruction of all remnants of the past. Down by the river, there were still some storefronts of the old river market from the days when junks and sampans crowded in so thick you could walk across the river on them. Beautiful, heavy-limbed trees climbed out of trim lawns that sloped this way and that, and whitewash and red tile mingled together in the shadows and brickle of sunlight. Everything looked newly washed or minted, and a stately air of English occupation softened the light.

On Friday night, we drove up to Newton Circus, the outdoor food market at the north end of the island. Crowds circled in and out of the stalls where steamed crabs were emerging from the cauldrons of the Chinese merchants who manned them day and night. We drank big bottles of Tiger and stuffed ourselves with crabs.

Some British Navy sailors befriended us and invited us aboard their ship; I was impressed that they actually served alcohol.

I walked around Singapore for much of Saturday. Singapore is a Saturday type of place, at least for me. I bought a watch and a camera. That was about all there was to do—that and read my Bukowski. (I'd brought his *Erections, Ejaculations, Exhibitions, and General Tales of Ordinary Madness*.) I found a Chinese teahouse, and I sat all afternoon, reading and drawing surf spots until it was time to start drinking.

The Marine Corps Birthday Ball is the time for things to happen that have been percolating for months. Most embassies turn over personnel in the summer because that is a convenient time for Americans to travel—kids are out of school and so forth. November, the time of the Ball, is about the time when people have become accustomed to one another and the embassy settles down. Because it is nominally a military event, people get all gigged up. In a place like Singapore, they come in kilts and uniforms and all kinds of get-ups.

We got dressed up too, me in a tux from Hong Kong, Sally in a sexy backless dress. Guys were smoking cigars, champagne was popping, and blue gin was splashing over ice cubes and onto the carpet. The Marines did their thing with the cake and the Commandant made announcements. I noticed the very attractive Woman Marine and remembered Ailbhis

Finn, aka Elvis. He must be here. Just then, a gaggle of women passed by on their way to one of their "let's all go to the restroom together" things; a collective head call. They were talking about someone and one of them said, "I've seen him before. I think he's an actor."

Another piped up, "No, he's a director."

"Anyway he's gorgeous," said an older woman. I looked over to where they had been and saw Elvis holding forth with a small group of people miles above his economic rung, and working it to the max; he clearly was the one the women were talking about.

He had them transfixed. Not wanting to disturb his moment, I walked around the back of the group facing him and raised my glass. He saw me and cut himself short, handed his glass to some guy, and came straight over, leaving his entourage watching him go.

Some of his audience followed him. "Hello Cunt!" he shouted, remembering my name, and he laughed his Hoo Haa laugh. "Let's go for a pint with the Marines later."

After the ball, at a little pub along the main shopping street, Elvis told me that Britain was going to war in the Persian Gulf. Wasn't there always a war over there? How could a war "start"? Wasn't it permanently underway?

Of course, I knew in general that things were heating up, but who was going to attack first? Meanwhile I was thinking, this guy is awfully well informed for a travelling hippie. How does he know this before me? Aren't I the CIA guy? The answer was that probably I would be the last to know anything.

He said he'd heard that the United States was leading a major military effort against Saddam Hussein, aimed at removing him from Kuwait and the face of the earth. The Marines we were sitting with had opinions about this, most of which involved staying in Singapore and screwing Chinese girls.

Elvis was planning to come to Jakarta on his way to Bali, and then head down to Australia and work in the wild country as a cowboy. I told him about Stretch and suggested he talk to him about all that Australian stuff.

Sally was in a sweet, drunken, affectionate mood. We went home and slept together, the first time we had done that. I flew out on Sunday to Jakarta, back to where you close your mouth in the shower.

At home, I settled into a routine of nights in the bars and days at the embassy writing cables and trying to look busy. I got out and around the city by working my Surveillance Detection Routes (SDR) all over town.

This meant taking three cabs, each going in a different direction, using choke points, and all that Farm stuff except putting a paper bag over my head and dancing like a chicken to get to my destination.

The harbor was a filthy fucking place, but it had a marina with some sailboats, so it might hold some promise of surf travel. I would have to get to know those sailors somehow.

I dreamed of having a little boat to explore the islands, but I figured I would really have to know what I was doing. Word had it that the Indonesian government would take a short cut when closing down oil platforms in the sea, simply cutting off oil pipes at surface level rather than pulling them up and out. I'd hate to run into the remains of one of those mothers going ten or twenty knots in a fiberglass boat.

I also got the feel of Chinatown and the markets in North Jakarta during the day and the Jaya Pub and Tanamur discos in the evenings; but I would always end up close to home, down at the Blok M bars, where the usual whores were always part of the scenery. Occasionally a new girl would show up and begin to do the rounds, but mostly the same old tired-out ones were looking for trade in Betty's Place and Top Gun.

The agent meetings were unexciting, and it was a far bigger challenge making sure you were following all the rules than getting intelligence out of the recruited agents. The American approach is to establish a major bureaucratic relationship with a person, rather than just buying intelligence from them, and during this epoch the review process was incredibly burdensome.

It was also becoming clear that the Agency liked to recruit people like itself, that is nice suburban people of host country nationality, who might have been candidates for employment back home had they grown up there. Even as far away as I was from holding opinions as to how things should be done, this appeared to me to be a mistake. I coined the phrase, "If you want to stand up with fleas, you must lie down with dogs," which I thought was kind of clever and also apt, though nobody ever laughed when I said it. But for the most part I wanted to go along and get along, so I didn't make a big deal about it.

What was clear was that these junior IBM salesmen types, whether male or female, were for the most part using tried and true conventional mechanisms to build their stock of recruitments, rather than going after tougher targets or less obvious hunting grounds. Of course they were. We had to recruit in order to get promoted, just like salesmen, and we had to follow the rules, of which there were increasingly many. I also didn't like the fact that people like Larry Ridge seemed more interested in playing it safe than in carrying out a mission. It wasn't my business and, again, I didn't have any brilliant ideas or reform strategies as I was very distracted by earthier matters, so I kept my head down and dressed like everyone else in short-sleeved Brooks Brothers shirts and khakis, and tried my best to look like I was just another guy who came to the Agency as an alternative to IBM.

Substantively, intelligence was the last thing on my mind (take that any way you like). I had no interest whatsoever in the issues of internal Indonesian politics and whether the Mullahs had any chance of winning against Golkar next time, or what the most likely presidential succession scenario would be. And as far as using the famous CIA tradecraft went, it wasn't really fun, like it should be. Sometimes you could kind of dress it up to be more dramatic, but basically you were using public transportation to get around a hot city and dealing several extra times a day with traffic because of the SDRs, suffering quick changes in temperature from the tropics to the icebox AC of shopping centers and hotel lobbies, and then meeting with bureaucrats or other types who were recruited by guys like Farley or Krebs and don't have much to say but are very polite and obedient and generally manage to always have a report to file. You then go into the office and write it up, along with all the accompanying paperwork. A long way from James Bond.

About this time, I was finally introduced to the diplomatic cocktail circuit, and I learned that Larry, my Branch Chief, had stalled and tried to keep me off it. I guess he figured I would embarrass him. I went to a Vin d'honour, which is one of the many forms of diplomatic ("dip") event, and there were the Americans I had been seeing around the embassy, a little more dressed up, and still looking frumpy alongside the Frogs and the other Europeans.

I passed out my card and learned my social standing was not very high as a Second Secretary. The United States sends so many people overseas that we dilute the impact of our diplomats, and, frankly, I was a nobody. Repeatedly, I would hand my card to an Indonesian gentleman who was invariably dressed in a formal batik shirt and sipping Kool-Aid, and he would squint at the card and put it away in his pocket and tell me he knew the former Ambassador Wolfowitz (a Jew, interestingly), who had been the greatest ever American in Indonesia, which was not particularly helpful now.

At events where the Indonesians were the hosts, there was never any alcohol. It was pretty pathetic. So I would make an appearance at these events, and, after a decent interval, head to Blok M, stopping at home to dump my clothes off and put on my jeans and cowboy boots (which were very useful on Jalan Pelatehan, what with its potholes and puddles everywhere), then make the rounds from the Top Gun end of the Street, via Betty's Place, to the wind-up spot at Tambora, rejoicing in the relaxed atmosphere free of pomp and the possibility of being seen screwing up by the scrutinizing eyes of my fellow Americans. Here in Blok M, I was the ambassador.

The news about Kuwait had not had much impact. Actually we didn't know what was going to happen next, just that there was far more interest than previously in Islamic groups. Things were routine. Krebs and Farley were golfing with the usual government and military types and promoting themselves in the front office, and my relationship with them had the superficiality of my distance in rank to them. After all, what could I possibly do to help either one? Plus, we were judged on our own merit, not as a team. It was a standard American machine. We sat at our desks, came and went on operational tasks, went home to our families, or, in my case, to Blok M, and on the weekends we went to the American Club, or, in my case, to the beach whenever possible.

The closest beach to Jakarta with surf is Pelabuhan Ratu, directly south on the Indian Ocean coast of Java. To get there is a three-hour journey, the first hour of which you are still in Jakarta, after which the ground rises into the Sunda district of

West Java, and you are transported into a tropical and mountainous region with an accompanying and abrupt slowing of the pace of everything. You eventually hit the coast, which is banked by the absurdly lush landscape of a South Sea island. To accomplish this journey, I would need a car. After looking at several, I bought a fifteen-year-old Peugeot as my surf wagon. I also planned to buy a jeep at some point, but this would be a good commuter and traveler.

I had noticed a guy hanging around my household, in the servants' quarters where Parto and his wife lived. My servants were apparently very distinguished in their circles, and I left them alone to look after me as they saw fit, which meant the house was clean and never robbed and there was always food to eat, usually *nasi goreng*, which is what they lived on most of the time. The guy was a cousin of somebody in their family, and he had just been kicked out of Mullah school, which meant two things to me: first, that he would never be a Mullah, and second, that he might make a good driver. So I hired him to do that, and I never made a better move.

This guy, Mas (meaning "brother"), had the uncanny ability to wait for me while I went into a shopping center or massage parlor or wherever, and to be exactly where I needed him when I came out. He got so good that I would test him to see if I could screw him up by coming out another door, but for the most part he was always there, leaning on the car smoking a *kretek* clove cigarette, waiting for me.

My entourage took awhile to assemble, but eventually I had a driver, a loyal guard, and a vehicle, which allowed me to sack out in the back seat while I, the precious cargo, was transported from one appointment with destiny to another, be it a bar, massage parlor, or Burger King.

When the weekend came, I set Kamal up like a California surfer. I gave him a longboard, my old 9'6" Hobie, which had arrived with my furniture. He already had invested in a jeep, an old Land Cruiser, and he was totally insane.

The plan for the weekend was to depart Jakarta on Friday afternoon. As sunset approached, we would plod up the mountains through the old city of Bandung, and past the massive volcano, Gunung Gede, whose gentle slopes form a steady decline as you move south from the spine of Java. As darkness approached, we would roll through the jungles of Sukabumi toward the Indian Ocean.

Kamal showed up totally wasted. I figured I had better start drinking right away to catch up. We put a cooler of beers in the back of his jeep and took off, weaving through traffic and driving up on the shoulder, taking full advantage of his diplomatic tags, with Sid Vicious and *Too Drunk to Fuck* blasting out the traffic.

He was telling me about picking up Albanian farm girls when his father was the Turkish ambassador to Albania. Kamal would take the girls up in the hills in a chauffeur-driven car, then have the driver wait while they took a nature walk.

Suddenly he stopped the car, saying, "Wait a minute, I have to puke." He did so, then kept driving and talking, yelling instructions to me on how to get laid in Paris and London, weaving all over the road and cranking the stereo.

I was pretty drunk myself by this time. A few miles south of Bogor where the traffic thinned out, I stood on the jeep's running board, reached out, and smacked a rearview mirror as we passed a car at around thirty miles an hour. The mirror, to my surprise, exploded in pieces. I hardly felt it. The car caught up to us and started honking and trying to pass. Kamal just kept cutting them off and finally they had enough and left us alone. Then suddenly, there they were again. They slid past and tried to cut us off. We got past and I started lobbing beer bottles back like depth charges on the road behind us. The first one landed just in front of their headlights and burst up into their windshield. After three depth charges, the enemy backed away. Timing is everything with depth charges.

Half an hour later, we were standing next to the car trying to explain this to an Indonesian cop. The enemy car had picked him up from his village along the road and brought him to us. We both could hardly stand up, and we would have broken a breathalizer. The cop didn't know what the fuck to do. We were very friendly to the enemy drivers, who managed some English, although we were drunk and treating them like old buddies from some Paris/Dakar rally. "How 'bout those depth charges?" "Timing is the key, huh?"

Finally Kamal had enough and started yelling at the cop, saying he was the Turkish ambassador and wanted to see the cop's boss, the village headman, the chief of police, and Suharto. Kamal pulled out his dip carnet and pointed to his CD license tags. Not that it mattered, we had won, but as he did this his revolver fell out of his boot and landed on the foot of one of the enemy drivers, who nearly jumped into my arms. The cop had enough and signaled for the enemies to take him back to the village.

We stumbled into the Buana Ayu Hotel around nine p.m. and got a split room with a curtain dividing an alcove from the main portion, like a hippie apartment. We were dancing around singing when we realized we needed to have dinner. Kamal had been to Pelabuhan Ratu before and had a favorite Chinese seafood place right in front of the port.

"Port" was an optimistic name, as it really was just a bunch of fishing boats pulled up on the beach. I called the restaurant the Botulism Basilica because the place looked like a Buddhist temple. After dinner, we took a drive to the "Monkey Market," Pasar Monyet, five miles up the coast road for more beers and whores.

By day, the Pasar Monyet is a respectable beach parking area with a number of grass-roofed kiosks selling soft drinks, beer and satay. The setup lends itself to nocturnal commerce. Ten or so kiosks transform into mini discos al fresco, and the girls circulate between the benches at the kiosks to parked cars and nature walks in the palms.

We drove straight through the parking lot and onto the beach, where we parked and opened up the back, set the cooler on the tailgate, and cranked the stereo. Soon enough, we were a kiosk. The girls came over and kicked off their shoes and Depeche Mode was rocking their stockings, even though they had never heard it before. We danced and drank beer and flirted, with intermittent moonlight illuminating the scene momentarily between clouds. A warm breeze was sucking the heat from the land, and the girls were trying to score with us. Finally, we succumbed, taking our selections back to the room.

Kamal picked a sexy one. She obviously had Chinese blood. Mine was less so, but smart and liked to laugh. It was very late and we were all pretty much nackered out, so I wasn't expecting much. My date and I took the alcove and drew the curtain. I was in a laughing mood. More accurately I was having a laughing fit. The chick was doing the same, but I wasn't going to give her twenty bucks for laughing, so we tried to mess around, but were pretty unsuccessful. Instead, we conspired to spy on Kamal. We sneaked to the curtain and looked through. The girl was on her knees, and he was screwing her from behind, swatting her on the ass and whispering obscenities to her. We were behind the curtain giggling. He kept going, getting rougher; she was groaning and moaning and giving little shrieks. They were not far from us. I grabbed my girl and started tickling her. Suddenly, we were falling. I grabbed the curtain or she did; anyway, we fell right on top of the happy couple, interrupting their lusty goings on.

That was it. The curtain refused to be re-hung; Kamal was pissed; my girl and I were worthlessly silly; and I think nobody got laid that night. Early in the morning, the girls left together and Kamal finally spoke to me around noon. The curtain was rehung while we were at the beach, and Kamal demanded the alcove for Saturday night.

We would surf at three spots. The hottie on this coast of South Java is called Cimaja. It's no secret spot, sitting across a rice padi from the coast road. There is a homestay right there, with an *ibu*, an Indonesian mother, who put out a good *nasi goreng*.

In the morning, you walk across the padi on little levees of clay to a cluster of palm trees on a round stone beach. It was cool to see people walking on the little levees, carrying boards—girls, surfers, walking out to the beach in the lush green of Java. The people, the rice padi, the sea and behind, the huge mountain range, the volcanoes and the fertile green valley, palm trees swinging their grass skirts in the breeze: this was the beauty of Java, with those powerful greens and blues.

At Cimaja, a hollow right comes off a point and winds up in a little indentation of the beach fifty yards down the line. At four foot, the place is an excellent wave, fun for longboarding and makeable to a decent pull-out in front of the indentation. At six foot, it cranks, and it holds until about ten foot, but that indentation becomes a purgatory of shorebreak and rip; you want the right equipment at this size.

This is still the Indian Ocean, home to some of the larger groundswells sweeping the planet, powerful corduroy on the earth's wet surface. There is no land straight south except Antarctica, thousands of miles down, and to the southwest is the most open expanse of ocean anywhere on the planet. Much bigger, and this little point/shorebreak couldn't handle it. Of course, much bigger and we might not handle it either; you're not in Malibu anymore, Dorothy.

The other spot was in front of the big hotel up the coast road near the Pasar Monyet. This is the hotel where they keep a room always vacant waiting for the Queen of the South Seas, N'yai Loro Kidul. She became human, had a thing with the Sultan of Yogyakarta, and winged herself into the ocean. You're crazy not to listen to local lore like this, so you never wear green into the ocean down here, as she will grab you if you do. Enough Javanese are grabbed on a steady basis to prove it, although it is also true that swimming is not a merit badge sport down here. Out front, there is a decent beach break with some surprising power. There is also the hotel pool if you want to hang with the Dutch and Japanese vacationers and have drinks with umbrellas served with your lobster.

The hotel sits on the point of land at the right end of a long sand beach. Up the beach, you can see the port of Pelabuhan, the boats with their painted *prahu* bows pulled up on the sand, and the fish markets where you can buy a shark. When there is a good swell, the break in front of the hotel in Pelabuhan peels off a little right hander along the seawall. That is pretty cool, especially if the balcony of your room looks right out over the break, and you just go down the path and you're in the water.

We did Cimaja first, but it was beginning to blow out. I got a couple of decent takeoffs back in the bowl, but mostly just came over the top because the cove was looking squirrelly. After one wave I got stuck in there for what seemed like a decade, unable to get out, and unable to get in through the shorebreak. We cooled off for a while on the beach there, which is a cool little isolated surfy scene.

Surfing the C.I.A.

Some guys land some beautiful ladies here. One Aussie was there with this leggy thing who looked totally Javanese but spoke Aussie style, so I gather he imported her. Probably they come and go and her family is in Indonesia, or maybe her dad is there or who the fuck knows. She was smokin, and the guy was cool, although he was a kook and nearly killed me by taking off on a wave and falling on his ass when I was paddling out. The beach was made up of smooth, round stones. You could create an indentation for your butt and put a towel down there and it was like having a chaise lounge to sit in.

Kamal dug stories about California, so I told him about my bro the "Dogman" who worked as a lifeguard at the Bel Air Bay Club in Santa Monica. He used to sit in the lifeguard tower with his shades on and look out the windows at the sea. Normally when he was guarding he was either stoned to the bejeesus or asleep, but when he was awake he would sit there, his body concealed by the shack walls, and he would be screwing his girlfriend, who was on her knees in front of him, keeping his thousand yard stare and gameface on.

In the afternoon, we drove down to Pasar Monyet and right back out on the beach. There were some people around, little crowds of Javanese and tourists here and there. We pulled up the jeep and cranked up the Beach Boys and danced around the car, and then crashed out in the sand for a while. The swell was picking up, so I wanted to try our hotel break for some smooth little right hand waves in the late afternoon.

Back at the hotel, Kamal returned to the room to have a massage from an old Javanese woman. I walked onto the veranda and stared at the sea. The waves were the only hint of the tradewinds outside the mouth of the bay. The veranda tiles baked in the afternoon heat and it seemed it could never be evening, nor morning, nor cool again. I watched a group of Germans walking on the beach. They came from bungalows in the distance, up the sand, and when they arrived at the rincon, where the cliffs stood, they could go no further. They stood together in a circle talking among themselves. They were perspiring, and they looked as though they had not anticipated having to stop, although they must have seen the cliffs and the rincon from far up the beach. The blue seas cracked on the point beyond them, and spray rose high into the heat. The red noses of the Germans caught the light and they turned to survey their path, hands on their hips, large ruddy bellies protruding above legs that seemed designed to hold up smaller loads.

Soon the Germans had gone. Other strollers came and went as well. The sun receded further and the trees seemed to grow as their shade marked late afternoon.

A waiter approached me where I was sitting watching the sea. "Mister mau apa apa?"

"Bir," I told him. He returned and disappeared again. I poured my beer and drank, sweeping the coolness back with my tongue and cheeks to where I could get all of the flavor. The foam rinsed the roof of my mouth and a feeling of calm content slid sideways into me. First came the rinsing, as though dry dirt were being washed away by cool water. Soon after came the warm and pleasant sense of an alteration, as though a pilot lamp were lit in my head. It was a strange and pleasant afternoon, the first time I had felt relaxed in Indonesia. Strange Spanish music played over scratchy speakers, and I could hear the noises of the town as dusk came on. I felt grateful for the sudden sense of peace, and grateful that I could be here and feel this way, slightly nostalgic and getting high and gazing out over the Indian Ocean.

Down the coastline, the sun shifted and shadows changed to glare and back again, the pattern different each time. In the dusk, men worked their *prahus* up the sand, their sails now flaked with the masts drawn together like fans. Out on the bay, more boats approached and men ran down to the sea to unload the catch. These were not fishing boats, but really cargo carriers that bring in the fish from platforms that are manned all night with many hand lines.

I stood near the edge of the veranda and looked out toward the tiny port. I thought of all I had seen here so far, and how my life was changing. This Indonesia I was seeing seemed so different from life at the embassy. I thought of Jakarta. I remembered some words I had read somewhere a long, long time ago and who knows what they were from: "Night falls. I sit alone in the dark, red city."

Chapter Six

The next trip (I was learning the key was getting out every weekend) would be Bali. I had been in Indonesia six months and had never been to Bali, so I bought a ticket to go. Nobody else was available, so I set myself up with a homestay in Kuta. I had heard about Bali and knew I would get some surf, although I wasn't sure if I could handle the extreme scene at Uluwatu or Padang Padang. It would be my last trip before my life, and my identity, would get more complicated.

    The plane came in low from the west, across the Banjuwangi channel that separates Bali from Java. It came in right over the waves and over guys taking off on some long rides in a kind of Waikiki type of scene just south of Kuta. The waves weren't fast, but it looked like nice, fun, easy, girl-friend-teaching kind of surf, fun for longboarding. The beach looked pretty cool. I really didn't know what to expect. By now I was fairly accustomed to Indonesia as a place to live, and I half expected Bali to be like, I don't know, Hawaii.

Off the plane and out of the airport, I immediately realized that this might as well be Java. The traffic zoomed past in every incarnation of internal combustion imaginable: motorcycles, mopeds, *becaks*, motorized this and that, trucks and cars of every description, all honking and smoking and burping and wheezing just like in Jakarta, Surababaya, or Palembang. This was Indonesia, not Hawaii.

The difference between Bali and Java became apparent as the taxi approached Kuta—I saw that some of the operators of this embarrassment of gasoline-driven gabble, some of the faces looking out of this petroleum exhaust stampede, were Western. I caught glimpses of decidedly Caucasian features and complexions everywhere, from cars and buses to motorized skateboards. The mass of motorbikes at a traffic light would include the usual dusky-faced locals, but one-third of the drivers nudging forward into the intersection were blond-haired Aussies or Dutch wearing sarongs and Balinese batik, their arms bearing tattoos from Sydney or Soho, and their bodies sometimes wearing the brand-name beach shorts and T-shirts from surf companies in California.

As we got into Kuta proper, the surf-town atmosphere intensified. T-shirt shops and pizza joints, surf shops and bars, restaurants of every description appeared on both sides of the street. The beach front in Kuta was a mad scene of surfers, bare-breasted Aussie girls, hippies on bicycles, taxis, cars, and a procession of Hindu priestesses carrying offerings down to

Ulu Watu. Hotels were everywhere, as was construction. In vacant lots, Brahmin cattle grazed and youth was everywhere: surfers, hippies, partiers, Europeans in the rag trade, local Balinese selling everything from wooden carvings to T-shirts. Wild, Wild Kuta.

I had arranged a homestay in the house of a friend of someone I knew from Jakarta. Her name was Bina, and she had come to Bali from Java after studying fashion design in Italy. The rag trade was built on the legs of old women who pedaled away hour after hour on ancient Pfaff and Singer treadles, needles perforating the foreign garb, which they indulgently created to Bina's exacting standards. At the end of the day, they would raise from their benches and march home, back up the mountain, in their traditional Balinese attire, untouched by Western product marketing strategies, and constructed to their *own* exacting standards.

Bina had really hit a vein. These ladies were lifelong seamstresses who worked for nearly nothing. Her influence was to endow the finished products with marketability far away where they fetched much higher prices. Buyers from Europe would come through, buy the designs, screw the models, whether male or female, and place their orders. Bina would cut the patterns, and the old gals would pedal away for pennies.

Rag trade buyers were not hotel guests. They were more inclined to come to Bali for months at a time, stay in a house—for free if possible—and party the whole time. It was a cool scene, exotic and erotic all the way around, with gay and straight crossing all over each other—the dusky, giraffe-like

Javanese models getting screwed by Italian studs, European girls with sunburns getting screwed by Balinese studs, Italian studs getting screwed by Balinese studs . . . girls girls, boys boys, Gypsy Kings and U-2 knocking people around on the dance floor, and an eliteness, a separateness from the whole world.

The taxi dropped me off north of Kuta in Legian, at a house that was kind of Bali-Spanish style, white with a sloping roof of red tile. Great wooden windows faced the road while the sides and back of the house faced into jungle.

An old *ibu* ushered me inside, where I immediately met Bina and Candy, a guy who looked like a Tahitian prince. They were massaging one another on a daybed in the airy main room of the place. Everyone was friendly; everything was cool. "You in Bali now," they said.

Bina and Candy showed me around Legian, then we headed to the beach. Once there, it was Brazil all over again. There were people from everywhere playing fresco-ball with its small hard ball and paddles, volleyball courts full of tall Scandinavians, Japanese, French hotties, surfers, models. It was a relaxed, late afternoon, and my board never made it out of its bag.

I went in the water, then dried off in the warm sand while my new friends told me all about Bali and why it is so different. They explained how the Javanese have tried to take over but can't, how the Muslims drove the Hindus out of East Java, and how the last Balinese soldiers committed suicide *en masse* rather than be conquered by the Dutch. Obviously the place was on the circuit for tourists and Euro-trash, Americans and Japanese, but it was mellow and everything seemed buttered and smooth somehow. The place just is.

As evening approached, we went back to the house and I had a cool *mandi* in the outdoor bath, where you scoop up water in a large dipper and pour it over your head. Bina went first and just smiled when I saw her nude. I gathered Candy was gay, but it seemed to be all mixed up here among the sexes, with nobody worrying too much about whose hands or lips were on them.

We met more people for dinner, and a long, European-style night emerged, with people looking elegant in their tropical attire, French wine and candlelight. After dinner, we moved to the disco and the party spilled out the back door onto the Balinese beach. People set up candles to mark off an area and sat talking in small groups and sipping cocktails in the sand.

It gave the impression of a fairy tale world in which everything is beautiful and easy, soft and pliable and dreams come true regularly. That night I slept alone, half thinking Bina might wander into my room, which raised the concern that maybe Candy would try something, saying, "You in Bali now."

I got some waves out front the next morning, and eventually got to surf the hot spots on Kuta side—Padang Padang and Uluwatu. These breaks, as legendary as they are, didn't turn me on that much. They were famous and crowded even in 1990, and there were stories of the "black trunks," tough locals who brought a California-style hostility to the waves.

Something about Legian had given me a narcotic dose of the mellows, and in the afternoon I went back up there to bask in it. I never made it back to the famous breaks; instead, Bina showed me around the island in her jeep.

The intimacy I had expected emerged late in my second night there through a haze of red wine and hashish; afterwards, it was a flirtatious, playful affection, inconstant and charming, not something to rely on. Kind of a thing of the moment.

She didn't seem to be with anyone else, but she wasn't exactly with me either. I suspected she had a relationship with an Italian who was away, but there were so many people discussed who were away that it was hard to draw a bead on who it might be. It didn't seem to matter to me either, as I was being seduced by the island magic of Legian, where right outside the house there were rice padis and processions heading down to the water.

Like Brazil, Bali is full of sea myths and superstitions, rituals and rites involving flowers and candles and things. To understand Balinese Hinduism you must unfold it with the uniquely Indonesian history of the place, and in the spirit of the diversity of the archipelago.

I wouldn't say the Balinese are friendly, exactly, and yet the island beckons to the visitor like no place else. It is a place to have a home, to come to from far away and to stay for months as though visiting a spa town in the mountains, or a place with baths and hot springs or some other curative element.

Nicholas Ware

It is both strange and familiar, lingering between the remembered and the new, possessed of all the natural beauty of the other islands, and yet smoothed over like a stone on a beach of stones. It is a place of beauty and promise, a seductive female place, like the indentation below the navel of the feminine human form. (Speaking of the feminine human form, Bina conveyed to me a malady that I discovered back in Jakarta days later and that required two weeks of antibiotics to stop the puss seeping from my organ.)

Chapter Seven

It was Thursday, and I didn't know it, but I was about to be called upon to execute my most clandestine act thus far, which, by all accounts, was not very clandestine. Nonetheless, it was something most Americans don't get to play at: counter-surveillance of a meeting between a CIA officer and an Iraqi.

This would require me to use the disguise that had been custom created for me and issued in a dap-kit, a zippered bag designed to look like a shaving kit. It was really absurd; it consisted of a custom-fitted black and grey wig, thick dark glasses, and an assortment of mustaches in little plastic cases with wax paper in between them to keep them from sticking together.

Of course, using a disguise is not just a matter of putting the stuff on; we CIA guys knew better than that. It's actually far more important that you change your mannerisms, your gait, and your general demeanor. To do that, you must match your attire to your character and, like a method actor, get under his skin a bit. To do *that*, you really have to know how a guy with grey/black hair that looks like a wig, thick glasses and a mustache would act. I had no idea. So just fucking wing it, mate.

On this occasion, JR was going to make a cold pitch to an Iraqi diplomat. He was going to lure the guy to a shopping mall, where he would then lure him into a restaurant, then lure him to a table, and ask him to work for the CIA. How was JR going to do this? What would be his bait? Pussy of course. JR was no fool. The idea was brilliant.

We knew that our target, Mohammed Whatever, was actively trying to screw a small, brown girl by the name of Rati. We knew he had not been successful. So we had a young Indonesian girl phone up Mo, and tell him that she and Rati were at the shopping center with her boyfriend, Hans, a Swiss businessman. Mo was flirtatious, trying to tear off a piece of Rati's friend, but agreed to meet them. Slick, eh?

In comes Mo, right on cue, and JR, aka Hans, is there waiting for him with the line that the girls have gone off to a lingerie store and would be back shortly. JR has the challenge of revealing that he is actually American, not Swiss. Mo would not have agreed to meet with an American, but no Swiss citizen would be recruiting for the CIA.

Meanwhile, I am in the restaurant, dressed as God-knows-who, drinking coffee after coffee and waiting while JR cajoles the dude to a table. He finally did it. Of course, Rati and the other chick were nowhere in the area, and in fact Rati was probably in some hotel as the guest of some other gentleman. What goes around comes around.

But now things got really interesting. The meeting lasted about an hour and a half, well into the evening. JR was brilliant. He started the guy off slow with small talk, and I could see them laughing and chuckling about the girls' antics, Hyuk Hyuk. Then there was a kind of sigh and a silence for a moment while both men took each other's measure, or at least Mo took a long, kind of quizzical look at Hans.

Then JR got right down to business. While I watched, he drew the Iraqi into a ten-minute, heads together, conversation. The Iraqi took a couple of gulps of coffee during the delivery, but kept on going, nodding his head. I imagined JR was going on about what a tragedy that Iraq was at war, and expressing his sympathy for all Arabs. Then he drew closer, and the look on the Iraqi's face began to change. Now I knew he was getting down to it.

After a few more words, Mo got to his feet and threw down his napkin. JR, who rowed varsity at Harvard, was up next to him and, hands on shoulders, eased him back into his chair. The Iraqi accepted the gesture and listened to a few more lines before he had his say.

I learned later from JR that, first and foremost, Mo was pissed because there were no girls. Then, when JR revealed he was American, Mo didn't believe him, saying his English wasn't good enough; Mo thought he was being false-flagged by the Germans, from all we could gather. Mo, however, was under no doubt that he had been pitched by an intelligence officer of some stamp, and beyond being angry, he was kind of flattered. But it was really all about the girls. He thought they would appear, sooner or later, and wanted nothing to do with spying, nor war, nor anything that didn't have a vagina.

This guy was really the first serious target I had seen up close, at least in circumstances that would put him into the cross hairs of the CIA. This was the real thing, I thought, with that dawning feeling of one who has just realized what his job will entail. But surely, it seemed, this will always be my role; they would never have me do what JR just did, nor did I really think I would be up to it.

This was the big time, like paddling out at Sunset Beach in Hawaii, where the masses of ocean water marching in and breaking could easily founder ships. You really have to have your balls in order to be out there on a surfboard, not that I would know. When you watch Sunset Beach on film, you occasionally get a water shot that conveys the kind of hugeness that distills the hugeness of what the guys are doing. There are other places like this that even I had surfed, but JR had just paddled out on a big day at Sunset and, with no hesitation, he had paddled into the biggest set wave. I mean we were practically at war with these fuckers, and here is this guy, as American as a Saturday morning, sitting across the table working him. Bitchin.

JR sat for a minute after our boy left, as though he thought the guy might change his mind, and then, with a look that included me, surveyed the place, picked up his tab, and moved out. I was left there kind of an awkward bystander in a weird outfit, very impressed, but now tired of this scene just a little. I'm not much of a spy, I thought, then wisely put the thought away where it could not haunt me too much.

When I got out on the street, the tropical evening had turned the corner to night and things seemed strangely tranquil, as though the texture of regular things like the rush hour traffic were affected by the day's events as seen through my prism. There seemed to be less traffic than usual, and it was running fairly smoothly, without the normal tangles and honking. I was pretty far from home, and, via Surveillance Detection Route procedure, it would be a three-taxi-ride anyway, so I could stop for a beer enroute.

I took my first stop at one of the jillion little shopping centers near Kuningan, but didn't go in. I just got out of my cab and into another going the opposite direction down the same street, making a mental note of the three thousand *rupiah* I had given the driver. These SDRs were an accounting nightmare and it was always easy to forget, usually in my favor, exactly how much I had parted with on each cab ride, and then add any little purchases for a total to be taken from the revolving fund.

For the next cab ride, I decided to go down to Blok M and just have a quick look in the bars before heading home to get this gunk off my face and peel off the mustache with the assistance of alcohol swabs. It seemed a little risky to go into the bars with this getup on, but I wasn't going in, really, just having a quick look.

When I got onto Jalan Pelatehan, I quickly got out of the cab, having squared up with the cab driver while he was still going. It was still early, 8:20, and there wouldn't be many girls around yet, and probably nobody much, except maybe some oilies down at the Sportsman. I remembered that I had checked and double-checked my appearance and decided that nobody I ran into would be able to figure out who I was—not because the disguise was good, which it wasn't, but because of the basic question: "What is Gus doing in disguise?" Nobody expects the Spanish Inquisition. So buoyed by that heady piece of philosophy, I marched right into Top Gun and took a bar stool in what I reckoned was the dimmest light.

I was no longer thinking about the day's events, being fundamentally far too selfish to look beyond how they affected me. I was, however, tired from the experience, and from not having been able to go home after work and take a siesta in the hammock or on the cool sheets with the AC up.

I ordered a Tiger Beer, which has been shown in the research I have done to be the least damaging of those available around Southeast Asia in terms of the next morning's headache, so when it is on the bar list I'm usually available to it. Tiger, like Bintang, comes in a big liter bottle. I was well into my second one without incident when the day's real action began.

It started out normally enough. While I was sitting at the bar talking to a whore I had seen a few times but had never spoken to, the place suddenly began to fill up, the way bars do in the most unpredictable rhythms. I checked my mustache, which seemed to be stuck on okay, and the girl didn't seem to have the slightest doubt that I was the geek I must have looked like, but then I guess her professional experience has built in a degree of suspension of disbelief, and she didn't look like the type to be too fussy.

We were having a very interesting conversation, with a few jokes thrown into it. Prostitutes have a great range of humor and we were exercising that. I was beginning to think she was not at all bad looking.

Down the bar were two Australians, pretty obviously surfers, having a conversation about the south-facing coast of Java and boat trips up to Sumatra. I thought kind of passively about asking them about the boats, but I was so strangely dressed I decided it was not going to happen. The south coast of Java is surf starred, with remote points and beaches facing the Indian Ocean and massive swells running for much of the year.

If the coast of Java is remote, the Sumatra coastline and its islands are more so, and the great chain of islands off that coast was clearly full of waves. In later years, the Mentawai chain would be exploited by surf adventure purveyors, and surfers from everywhere would pay varying rates for varying accommodations aboard varying qualities of vessels and spend weeks at sea along those islands, just far enough out to avoid malaria from the mosquitoes that inhabit the islands. The area already had surfers, but it still was not genuinely explored. These two Aussies were the first I had heard speak beyond speculation about the breaks outside of the usual Bali and Java spots, and Nias, to the north of the Mentawai chain.

I was particularly curious about Java, because it was possible I would be able to get someplace interesting by car. A spot called Desert Point was mentioned, and I thought I knew where that was located. Then they went on, in that drawl so charming to Americans, about the Ujung Kulon Park, at the lower western tip of Java. That sounded accessible, then not so, as their conversation lilted forward in the quick frame mode of surfers, but with a slightly different eloquence that indicated a more sophisticated speaker and listener than you get at the usual punk rock concert in Orange County.

I gathered one of these guys was a geologist working for an oil company. His rig sounded like a much-enhanced Land Rover with a major surfboard rack and an inflatable dinghy on the roof. The other guy did something or another in Jakarta, but they had both been all over Indonesia. I felt like a kook listening to them.

I began to notice that Yanti, the whore at my side, had very round, and not altogether small, breasts, unlike the usual girl who was very nearly flat chested. That had never mattered to me before, but a prurient curiosity now engulfed me, threatening to dislodge my attachment to the lower portion of a woman's physiology, rather than the upper. This preference for the nether region is partially a result of my early years in Brazil, where the buttock serves as a woman's marketing division, and partly from my American side, which is pure Yankee practicality: the breasts of course, possess no useful orifice.

About this time, I was able to identify another small problem—my speech was slurring noticeably; fortunately not much was expected of me in my current company. I therefore continued to talk with Yanti, moving the conversation slowly toward the prospect of her exposing her nipples to me at some indefinite point in the future or perhaps sooner than that.

As I became more brazen, I was also becoming more curious about the Aussies and their surf safaris. Had they known another surfer was sitting at the bar, of course, their discourse would have been postponed or relocated to more discreet surrounds. It was possible to become friends of course, but that would take time; the surfing world was already so crowded that these pioneers kept their own counsel and worked to keep their spots secret as long as possible. Americans are also somewhat suspect on the Aussie surfer/pioneer circuit, because they always seem to have friends who want to make a business out of a spot. These guys, from what I could gather, were pretty cool, and were really looking for surf and adventure out there on the edge.

I met the eyes of one of them. He studied me for an instant, then looked back toward his buddy, who was speaking. I remembered I was in disguise, but this seemed to matter less now that it was night, and after all these were Aussies, not Arabs. So I started to get my pluck up to insinuate my way into their conversation. Beer is proof that God loves us.

I should have had a mirror with me, and unfortunately there was none in the *weh-ceh*, as the restroom is called in Jakarta. A disguise is like the polygraph exam, in that it works with a physical manifestation, but is only effective through a human element. The polygraph examiner watches his subject carefully, and also observes the gyrations of the needle, the stimuli and response. A disguise, when endowed with an actor's humanity and the changes that entails in the wearer, can render one unknowable to one's own parents. With enough beer, however, one can begin to act like himself while looking like someone else. This has the effect of really goofing up the process, with the result that actions and appearance don't blend and allow you to avoid attention. Instead, as I was beginning to learn, you attract attention.

When I returned from the mirrorless head, an oilie had positioned himself on the other side of Yanti, between her and the surfers, and was speaking to her on some urgent business. He would say something to her and look over at me with what I took as his version of disgust.

Fights don't occur much in these bars, and are seriously discouraged, although among the *bulehs* there was the occasional scrap and at least one business-related homicide in the past few years. I wasn't thinking of violence in the least, just trying to see past the oilie to read the surfers' lips or to catch a phrase from their palaver.

I heard the oilie say hello to them, in a too-familiar tone, and tell them he was from Texas. They looked back at him, the way the one surfer guy had looked at me before, but were polite enough to say hello and get back to their conversation. The more I heard, the more I liked these guys, and the more I wanted to get into the discussion. At this point though I was also interested in Yanti, and felt some competition coming from the squat oilie from Texas, who clearly had his eye on her.

"It is strange to be in competition for a commodity that was so democratic in its economics," was the last thought to pass through my mind before I felt my barstool lifted up and me with it and the Texan's right fist hit the left side of my head. I didn't see it coming because he had reached around in front of Yanti (recreating the incident later, I decided she must have had some complicity or at least didn't warn me) and gave me a very effective roundhouse to the temple and upper cheek. I landed on the floor by the front door of the bar. My wig was down over my face exposing very blond surfer-looking hair.

Both my arms were suddenly gripped by strong hands, and I was moved outside very quickly. It was the two Aussies, who took me out of the bar while the bouncers dealt with the Texan. They moved me down the block and around a corner into a side street where they propped me against a building and looked over my damage.

I was now holding my wig in my lap, and it was pretty clear my mustache had been knocked half off and my glasses were broken. I was also quite drunk and very surprised by my sudden change of perspective on the world—from sitting to lying to sitting again in another place, having never once utilized volition. I heard the accent again saying, "What's yer nayme, mayte?" and I gargled out Gus in response. "Raight, where from, Gus?"

"Bloody strainge gitup," said one to the other.

"California" was the penultimate word from my mouth before blackness overtook me. "Surfer" was the last.

One of the worst things about having been really drunk is not being so any more. If one were able to go through all of life in a state of total inebriation, there would be no reason to change anything, to get hung up on drugs or alcohol or anything.

Of course, the version of the story I relayed was only my own, and it apparently omitted a number of clever contributions I made to various conversations in the Top Gun, which were later related to me by my new Australian buddies.

It appears that while I had not made it into their conversation, I had conducted a few of my own with other patrons of Top Gun, and once Yanti and Tex had sealed their evening plans I had gotten quite a bit further into their conversation than I remembered. I had also defiled Texas with my tongue, saying there were only two things that came from there, etc. In other words, I had done everything but pay the guy to punch me.

It appeared that for a certain window I really had been the life of the party, playing air guitar and singing "Uncle John's Band." It was also now clear that I had been pretty much revealed in the place as being in disguise, and that it was the talk of the town in Blok M that evening, although fortunately, I was referred to simply as "the moron," not by name.

The guys brought me around with ammonia caps, and gave me what appears to be the Australian remedy for headache: beer. By the time I was *compus mentus*, I was slouched in the back seat of the Land Rover, and we were heading away from Blok M. These two good souls, Phil and Nick, got me home, and I was put to bed by my servants. It was still before midnight and I was okay. I hadn't been punched in years and it was good to know I could take it.

Chapter Eight

The next week, I kept my head down, concerned that my profane finish of the day would suddenly rise up like a set of large waves coming over the horizon. I braced myself for the call to the front office. At this time I was still lingering in the naïve belief that the Agency had eyes everywhere. The truth was that nice suburban people and former missionaries don't hang out in sleazy Southeast Asian bars, and that is who made up the Station. I was still the only single adult there except for some old-maid secretaries, who would figure even less in that milieu. The simple fact was that I was safe in my ignominy; the Station would learn about such an event only if it made the press or the gossip circles of the American Club. So what came when I finally got the call to the front office was a surprise indeed.

Surfing the C.I.A.

I was distracted by some news on Indo in *Surfer* magazine so when I was called up front I temporarily forgot about that night. It came rushing back to me, however, as I managed the cipher lock to the Station Chief's office, and for an instant, I thought I was screwed.

The Station Chief was a former analyst with an amiable demeanor—kind of a learned-looking guy who got along well with most people. I don't know how effective he really was, being insulated from him by middle-management, including Larry, but he was always very nice in a mildly disapproving way, which showed me that the Chief was far more aware of what surfers get up to than the rest of the place. JR was in the office as well, with a grin that told me something was up, but that I was not in trouble. It seems he was not satisfied and would not be until someone in the place cuddled up to an Iraqi. I have often thought that my having been present at his cold-pitch was influential in my selection for this next deal.

"So, Gus, how good is your Spanish?" asked JR. The Chief was seated, looking me up and down. I wondered briefly if the Chief had ever been to Blok M and then tried to concentrate.

"I speak Spanish and Portuguese too," I told him. "My Portuguese is better because I lived in Rio for ten years, but my Spanish is also okay. I lived in Lima, Peru for three years," I said, forgetting that I was speaking to Americans who knew geography. "That was a long time ago, but it was fluent. Are we targeting Latinas?"

I started to smile at my attempt at irony, but it was overlooked as they looked me over. The Chief peered at some papers and propped his feet against his desk. He suddenly reminded me of morning TV's Mister Rogers, and I thought he should be wearing a cardigan—kind of an impractical garment for Jakarta though, maybe a college sweatshirt . . . he could turn himself into a kindly sort of Colonel Potter type from M.A.S.H. I thought he went to school at Duke or someplace, which would look good in raised print, and I began to picture his office studded with school banners and his college letter for bowling or debate or whatever, but I was now being spoken to again.

"Can you look the part of a Latino?"

I allowed that I probably could.

JR, it seemed, had come across some interesting news that was fodder for his strategic mind. Another Iraqi was about to travel back to Baghdad with the Iraqi Embassy's diplomatic pouch and we had somehow gotten hold of his itinerary. He would be leaving in two weeks, flying out of Soekarno-Hatta to Singapore, and then proceeding on. This would give someone a window of opportunity to meet him at the airport or on the plane. JR was not about to pass up this opportunity.

It both excited and sickened me to think the candidate for this op might be me. On the one hand, I thought, can't I just go quietly through this tour and fly neither high nor low, stay out of trouble and get some waves? On the other hand, I wanted to get in the game in controlled, safe way. In the end I decided that this was not very likely to succeed, and trying it for JR's sake was the best way to look like I had given it a shot; then, hopefully my number wouldn't come up again for a while.

Surfing the C.I.A.

I was dismissed from this meeting while the great minds consulted. I went back to my desk and stole a last look at my *Surfer* mag before stuffing it into my briefcase. This mag had arrived a month late, but I always welcomed it; I had grown up reading it late in South America anyway. Surf travel in Indo was still a whisper, although an excited whisper, and some exposure was inevitably coming our way. I wasn't worried about the article bringing crowds to the spots. I was here now, and it would be some time before the average surfer in Huntington Beach would get his act together to get over. Besides, there were so many spots and still relatively few surfers, and it would be available to me while it grew. Meanwhile, I had totally forgotten about the meeting I just had in the front office.

When it next came up, I approached the assignment with a feigned enthusiasm that probably looked a little crazy, but was designed to camouflage my basic panic at being placed in the spotlight. I was not even thinking of the Iraqis. The Station hierarchy would all be watching me float my little boat on its maiden voyage, and that would almost surely bring other aspects of my life into focus—a scary prospect considering I was pretty weird even by surfer standards.

I was particularly protective of certain hippie trappings of my life and only grudgingly divulged matters such as being a fanatical Deadhead. The reason for my "unlimited devotion" (a lyric) was pretty simple and fairly common in guys a few years older than me in San Francisco and, oddly enough, Lima.

The music of Jerry Garcia had nursed me back to reality during a particularly nasty acid trip at age fifteen, and I would be forever linked to that experience. You think you are a goner and that your mind is totally fucked for a few hours, and you grip reality tightly while the worst of it rises up and engulfs you. Finally, you have no choice but to let go, and by that time the LSD has so permeated your reality that nothing is real anymore and you might as well be dreaming. After the peak you begin to relax, and if you are lucky, like I was, you are among friends who know what music to put on. The Grateful Dead were famous in this psychiatric nursing role and probably saved many minds of people who went on to finish college, study law and run for office. Given the CIA's supposed role in introducing acid to California, it seemed ironic that one of theirs had been inserted into the Agency now. Anyway, I didn't publicize the fact and I kept my dancing bear stickers and my old top hat to myself, saying it's just a California thing. But now I was concerned that I would be exposed.

So I had some thinking to do about how I would go about building myself into a Latino, and exactly what stamp I would be. I was seriously considering Brazilian, feeling more confident of being able to pull that off in a greater variety of circumstances. The fact that I don't look like most people's idea of a Brazilian was no genuine obstacle, given the racial variety that exists there, what with ex-Nazis and other Germanics, especially in the south of the country, around Porto Alegre, where there are some excellent point breaks, by the way. The main problem was that Brazilians are cool, and I had no idea what my character would be like.

Surfing the C.I.A.

The file on the Iraqi was kind of like one of those dossiers you see on TV shows. It contained photos and background on the man and it had SECRET stamped all over it. We had some formal-looking photos of the guy, who was about my age, single or at least unaccompanied here in Jakarta. He looked like several of my childhood friends, Lebanese kids in Rio and others of Arab extraction. He actually looked like a nice guy, this enemy of ours. It made me wonder if somewhere someone was reviewing a dossier on me. Probably some American; maybe the Chief, or Larry more likely.

And so, it came to be, one rosy fingered dawn. The week arrived when I was supposed to try to make contact with this enemy of ours and, as though with molasses and flypaper, lure him into friendship with me. I spent a good part of the week trying to figure out a certain Latino look that had no doubt disappeared from all but the coffee table books of old Rio, a look that included men wearing hats and crisp white linen suits—suits that could be easily duplicated at any decent corner tailor shop in Jakarta.

I remembered seeing, as a child, from our balcony in Copacabana, white linen-thronged sidewalks with mosaics, big black swirls of tile being the only black apart from the skin of about half the wearers of off-white linen. One night my sister and I observed a man, so dressed, bury himself in the sand completely, but we were fussed off to bed by unbelieving adults and so ends that story. I would like to say we crossed the street and confirmed the event the next day, but I have no such memory. My mind skipped to the big house on Rua Fonte Da

Saudade and the glowing candles that we used to put in paper balloons, which we then released—a practice long-since prohibited for the fires it started, but still practiced. That's Brazil all right.

These memories came flooding back as I studied the role ahead of me and tried out different approaches in front of my full-length mirror. Disguises are actually fairly rarely used by American intelligence, yet I was into two within a couple of weeks. Unlike my role as the mustache nerd though, this time I was getting into costume rather than disguise, and I would be acting out a drama rather than trying to avoid detection.

This was by far the most interesting professional action of my life, and I was beginning to really put energy into it. That same week, however, I began to put some nocturnal energy into a girl I met at the home of the French Embassy's draft dodging interns (*les cooperants*). So as usual, my energies were split.

Agustina was an extraordinary girl for her sensitivity, love of fun, occasional poutiness, and, for an Indonesian girl, her hipness. She spoke a bit of French—she had been dating a French dude before I came along. I heard that he was a real fuck-about, so I felt no qualms in taking over his girlfriend while he was away in Paris.

Strangely enough she wouldn't put out, but I started seeing her nonetheless, breaking one of my strictest codes—perhaps my only one. She seemed happy to move on to an American, which surprised me a little. I have had French friends everywhere I have ever lived. For some reason I get along great with some Froggies, but they invariably have snotty Parisian friends who are just too cool for words and don't think much of me, or America. Anyway, the *cooperants* had a great house where a bunch of them lived, providing their embassy with assorted levels of service as an alternative to the Army. Some were really cool, others were foppish pricks, but it was like having a fraternity house in the middle of town, and it had a higher plane of pussy circulating around it than the Marine house did, as well as some decent Beaujolais Nouveau.

While this relationship was cooking, I would have to keep my distance so as not to screw up the job that kept me in the country. Eventually, I would have to face the issue of declaring to the Station that I was sleeping with a foreigner, since flag is everything. But that was still remote; I figured until I had sex with her there was no issue. So I kept her at a distance, calculating a later acceleration before her Frog got back from Paris. I figured, symmetrically, that after I had sex with her, the Frog would be no issue.

After my siesta, I spent some time dressing up like a spic and trying to sound foreign. I had still not decided what kind of Latino to be, but Brazilian (as in football and women's butts) was holding the deepest promise.

A distinctive element in Brazilian Portuguese is evident in the pronunciation of their country, which typically sounds like "Braziu." So I could pass myself off, with an anglicized first name and a Brazilian surname, the way ex-Nazis and train robbers have done, as Bill Santos, and be "Biu from Braziu."

I was zeroing in on a character for reasons beyond the operational, and inventing a personage of some means, in the hope this might lead to some fancy funding if the thing ever went forward, which seemed doubtful. Thus, I planned to be a kind of wealthy playboy from Rio whose yacht is circling the globe and whose family is interested in conducting business in the Middle East. This was about the best I could have done, and being pretty much a spoiled brat myself, the shoe really fit. I had spent years in Rio and could fool Americans there into thinking I was a local, so I should be able to pull it off with a raghead.

To get boringly technical, what was about to happen was a false-flag recruitment attempt (Chapter 5 of the CIA/Woody Woodchuck Manual). This technique is taught at The Farm, the CIA training grounds in Virginia, and is also described in any decent spy novel or movie. It simply means the U.S. hand will be hidden while it diddles the target, cloaked as it were, with the flag of a third country.

This perhaps explains why intelligence services say that there are no friendly foreign countries, what with Americans dressing up as Brazilians and Argentines dressing up as Englishmen and everyone trying to look Canadian. Actually it reflects the real world fairly well. Some countries conduct much of their foreign intelligence collection through third countries, having weak or non-existent intel services of their own. When they stumble, as when Americans appear on TV in Cuba filmed in the act of spying, it clarifies things a little.

Surfing the C.I.A.

Some countries can be counted on to spy all the time, like the United States, Russia, China, Israel—the biggies. What Brazil does about it is anyone's guess. I don't think they care that much about national security issues or threats. It would be foolhardy to invade Brazil anyway, and the invaders would probably get duped into paying off the national debt.

It is probable that Iraq was running intelligence operations of some kind, but we didn't know about them at that time, at least I certainly didn't. Their intel officers probably came from the Republican Guard or some other military background, and their roles were probably very specific. My target was a First Secretary and Vice-Consul, whose unhappy privilege it was to transport diplomatic mail and such in the "immune to scrutiny" diplomatic pouch.

I was prepared by JR, in the event of a last minute switcharoo by the crafty enemy, to look for another Arab-looking dude carrying some official-looking papers and perhaps a special type of briefcase. Americans, of course, make a big deal when they carry the diplomatic pouch. I think they make the most of the occasion and get the least, as they are so indiscreet with their obligation that everyone knows what they are carrying. Agency people seldom get chosen to carry the pouch, but it would be better for the country if they did.

Out I went to the airport, dressed as a rich Brazilian, which entailed buying a designer T-shirt and some loafers and acting the part. I combed my hair for this one, but kept my basic appearance intact.

I had studied the dossier, but I am immensely fallible, and at first thought I had got it all wrong. Maybe the wrong flight, wrong time, wrong airport? It was nearly flight time, and my guy was nowhere in the lounge. These satellite lounges protruded from a central lobby like lozenges sticking out on the tarmac, and each satellite lounge had its own restroom, down a flight of stairs from the seating area. Actually the rest room was served by two sets of stairs, kind of wide and open so as not to trap the air, in a kind of old fashioned tropical style, even though the entire airport was now air-conditioned.

I surveyed the crowd and decided my guy wasn't coming. It was nearly flight time now, close to the noon hour, and he should have been sitting there punctually waiting for the plane to depart; I was there, after all.

I spotted a frumpy, swarthy man who could been Brazilian as easily as Arab, and sure enough, he had with him a special looking briefcase, was consulting some official-looking papers, and looked every inch a carrier of diplomatic pouches. I sat down next to him and began to speak with my best Braziu accent. He was from someplace, for sure, but I couldn't get around to asking him where, for fear it would get his antennae up. But he was friendly and this was a breeze, and I thought wow, you're laughing now, Gus, just move it forward quickly because the plane is probably just a little late, and they will call you any second. I relaxed a bit, and took a sigh in a natural pause in the conversation. So I thought: switcheroo.

When I looked up from my watch, I looked right at my real guy, entering the satellite lounge and walking directly toward me. His gaze took me in with equanimity, despite the look I must have been wearing. He made an abrupt left. however, and descended into the washroom. I dumped my other new friend unceremoniously. He was obviously an imposter, poor slob, some insurance guy from Morocco or something. It then occurred to me to go have a piss in the washroom and somehow, through the general fraternity of those who pee standing, like at a ball game in the States, to say something funny to my neighbor while we pee. I should first say that this is, in general, a stupid idea. Neither speak nor listen to strangers whilst thou pee-eth, should be a commandment: "Neither a speaker nor a listener, whilst you pee, be," should be a proverb. It's just really weird to hear a friendly salutation while you and another male have your dicks out, so just don't.

Down I went intending to do precisely that. But Saleh, as this dude was known, was not available for that gambit anyhoo. Instead of pissing like a good American, he was over there washing his hands. Being a good American, despite my disguise, I peed, by which time he was outta there. I followed at a decent interval, not wanting to attract attention (fat chance of that), and as I trotted up the stairs, I planned to find him in the lounge, to sit down as close as possible and to just get this fucking thing over with.

With that plan in mind, I reached the lounge and found him deep in prayer, sitting up with the Koran on his lap and the Islamic rosary beads across his open palm. So that's why he was washing and didn't pee like a good American. The guy has religion. Okay, so now I had to wait, and it may come as a surprise that while I waited I thought of nothing brilliant to do or say. The only advantage I could see was that he had sat with his back to the desk of the ground personnel for this lounge. So I hatched an ingenious plan.

Muslims pray religiously, so to speak, at certain times of day or when circumstances merit. This guy was already having a pretty good day and had been sensible enough to call ahead to the airline, which informed him that the flight would be delayed. He was dialed in. I know this because he told me this after I executed my wickedly delicious ingenious strategy, which consisted of yelling at the ground personnel right through him as he was finishing his prayer.

Since he was finishing, he had taken no offense to my weird shouting, which went something like, "Planes are never late in my country!!" Yeah, Brazil, right. In fact, Saleh was grinning at me, as he took in my histrionics, and after a long look at me during which I gave the universal "scoffing at the incompetent ground personnel" look to him, hoping to elicit complicity, he impassively continued grinning and said to me, "Where are you from?" He was clearly very much amused by my Latin outburst.

Here was my first encounter, and I couldn't have said anything else. "Braziu, my name is Biu," I heard myself say. He looked like he thought that was the funniest thing in Christiandom or wherever, but he kept his cool and just looked at me, smiling and blinking. The conversation was far more natural than I could have anticipated. For one thing, it is easier to speak with an accent if your listener speaks with one as well. I could either resort to my Braziu stuff or simply mimic his trilled r's and intonations. Within minutes, we were both laughing at or with each other, and, as happens in the best dissembling, little truths were popping out all over, such as my guessing that he had phoned ahead and knew the plane would be late, and had taken his time getting to Soekarno-Hatta, but had left work early nonetheless.

He was very open about being an Iraqi diplomat, and told me directly that he was carrying the pouch back to Baghdad, and was concerned about the war and was glad to be in Indonesia, and had a wife and a son. I was already getting to know the guy so well I would have nothing to ask him soon except Saddam Hussein's hat size.

I did have a little problem, however. It was now clear the plane was preparing to board. A shimmer of movement was turning the passengers into herring flashing toward the jetway entrance. There was the customary standing up and folding of newspapers, the anticipatory knee-jerk preparations for departure and the accompanying competition to get someplace first, even if only the jet-way. There was some activity in the ground personnel booth, where they were now terrified of me and avoided my glances their way. They were moving and stepping up to the microphone; always a signal to sprint.

Soon we would have to board the plane and I would have to produce a Brazilian passport, which I didn't have, and show it to an airline officer. I had already identified myself as Mr. Santos to the ground personnel, and it was inevitable Saleh and I would walk to the jetway together.

As we began to move, I made a fuss out of dropping my suitcase and in doing so, I set a pick, as in basketball, by arranging matters so that a rather stout gentleman stepped very naturally between us, pushing the Iraqi along, followed closely by a mother with two screaming brats, she herding them planeward as though Jakarta were ablaze, so that he could not possibly stop and wait for me. He waved, and we made signs that we would speak again; he boarded the plane well ahead of me. Close one.

When I got up to the jet-way, the ground guy from Garuda was there and was saying to me that he was sorry for the delay, Mr. Santos, as he read my name as Mr. Hayes in my U.S. passport. He must have just decided not to ask; nuther close one.

Being a fairly observant young dilettante, I noticed Saleh taking a seat in about row thirty-five on the starboard side of the aircraft, while I was in about row fifteen to port. I decided not to wave to him (recalling my peeing strictures); instead, I would pop on back during the flight and get his phone number. To have come this far and not get a number was right out of too many bad Saturday nights, and besides, I was doing this for my country, not my penis, which meant it would be much easier.

My next problem came when they didn't take my food tray off me after the meal. The flight from Jakarta to Singapore is a brief one—up to a peak and down the other side in a little over an hour. It was nice of Garuda to give us a meal, but now I was stuck in my seat and the stewardess had gone AWOL or something. I waited patiently for justice to be done, but as usual, it wasn't. I finally stuck my tray in the aisle for her to trip over next time she came by and sashayed back to Saleh just as the announcement came on to take our seats and fasten up for the descent.

By now I was feeling pretty confident, so I draped myself over the seat in a very Brazilian way (they don't know how to sit uncomfortably and obey) and chatted away with my new bro. He was actually very comical with the edges of a witty cynicism peeking around the bend of this stranger-to-stranger talk. I relaxed my accent a bit, got his business card, on which he wrote his home number, and we said our good-byes. God help me if I would see him in the immigration line. I didn't, praise be to Allah.

Chapter Nine

I was suddenly the conquering hero, and everybody seemed to know it. While I was in Singapore, Sally proposed marriage to me, and I kind of sheepishly told her I would think about it, Sally being a great woman but lacking the variety offered by the fleshpots of Blok M. I hadn't told her exactly what was going on at work, but she seemed to sense some mighty achievement. I let her think so and shamelessly exploited the situation without much of a care for her, since I was a bit exhausted by what had happened and wanted some comforting (when didn't I want that?).

By the time I got back to the Station, everyone knew that I had gotten my man. I was suddenly someone. In the staff meeting that week, I was even asked my opinion on another operation about which I knew nothing. I blew my chance by saying I didn't know, but that didn't change matters. I had done a good job on what was becoming an important target.

Of course, I remembered from high school that when you move to the front of the class, you have to start doing your homework, and that was a bit of a problem. Anyway, for the moment I was golden, and I should get some slack if I screwed up now, so I had that for comfort.

I got a warm welcome in the bars. I even got an apology from the Texan guy, who said he wouldn't have punched me if he had known I was an American. I accepted his apology much in the way I had taken Sally's proposal. Since my disguise was not supposed to look American in the least, it appeared that I was pretty well made down on Pelatehan Street in Blok M.

Snake Woman was in fine form. Stretch was still trying to work her, and it had become a sort of joke between them. Stretch had also gotten to know Phil and Nick, who were outstanding blokes, and Kamal was as insane as ever. This week also saw the arrival of Elvis from Singapore. He moved into the Kebayoran house where he and Stretch shared the guest room or the couch, depending on their luck in the bars. Meanwhile, Agustina all but moved in with me. There are CIA rules against all of this stuff, of course, so I broke them.

Agustina came up with the idea for the party. It sounded good, and I thought I might even get some funding from the Station. I persuaded them that I would use it to make some new contacts, which was true enough. They gave me $100, which helped with the booze.

Agustina put herself in charge. Some friends who did lighting and stereo work crawled all over my house for a couple of days. I got a little worried that they might be planting listening devices, but I came home and they were all getting stoned and I forgot all about it. At any rate, I figured that anything said in this house might as well be heard, except by my own side.

When I got home from work on Friday, the house had transformed itself into some kind of disco palace garden. The party would be a kind of black dress luau Dutch orgy Bali swing sock hop. Orgies in Bali were known as "Sexy Parties," and everybody knew what was going on. It was strange that they got dressed up to go considering most of the clothes would come off. This party wouldn't match them, but it was going to be pretty slick.

The lighting kids were there until about nine o'clock and then everyone disappeared. At just before eleven, I was doubting if anyone would show up at all. I had been instructed by Agustina to wear my tuxedo, and because it was still crumpled in the backpack I had carried to Singapore, I wore only parts of it. Agustina had gone to get dressed with her friend, and I was sitting there alone . . . in the dark, red city.

Then they showed up. One by one the guests entered, slick black hair and dusky features, proud foreheads and aquiline noses, the elegance of Java unveiled. They wore black, with splashes of color in a cummerbund or gown, combs stuck into hair piled high on the heads of giraffe women, whose lankiness made them look taller and very slim. The kids who had wired the house for sound and light wearing jeans and shorts were transported into the land of wealth and elegance through the sleight of hand of fashion and taste. One who had hung lights high in the tree in the afternoon was now a young scion of Java, elegant in a double-breasted jacket and a black turtleneck. The roadies had become the rock stars, and they were coming out on stage to strut their stuff in feather boas and sequins.

I swam through the party gleefully, flirting and throwing out superficial greetings like a caricature of the Great Gatsby, transformed from my ordinariness as an embassy underling and spy-third-class to a wealthy landowner and playboy. I had no conversation lasting more than two minutes until the champagne did its work on me and mellowed my mood, and even then I behaved myself.

Agustina wasn't the jealous type, but things happen at this type of party, and inevitably somebody gets laid in the bathroom, which was constantly occupied throughout the evening. The girls were more beautiful than usual, running the gamut from the tall, slender, supermodel type to the more diminutive Javanese dancer, whose muscles give slightly more substance under their clothes. I had that special position of host, which makes a man so desirable to women, and I basked in the attention I was getting.

By midnight, I was dancing with a model a foot taller than me. She was one of those alien types, neck like a giraffe, smooth Javanese skin, hip bones thrusting forward under her dress indicating a concave pelvic area to which she was pressing me. I looked over at Agustina and saw she was watching me, grinning and wagging a reproving finger at me in mock censure. Now the girl was reaching inside my shirt and I was holding on to her upper legs. Suddenly she gave me a Javanese kiss called a *cium*, which means sniff, and broke away to dance with some other giraffe of her own species. I couldn't believe my eyes. This was not my house; this was not my yard. Giraffe were everywhere, and gazelle and wildebeests. Models, beautiful, exotic women like I had never seen. Nobody else seemed to notice. Agustina did though. I felt her behind me as she responded to my thoughts and whispered, "Dees call welcome to Indonesia."

I reckon most of the people there were on Ecstasy. The party went on and on. I even saw Snake Woman there. She looked like a model too, which may have explained a lot of things, and Stretch was escorting her as though they were an item. Elvis was in high form and wearing a kilt. Kamal was busy insulting an English girl, and the Aussies were hunting giraffe.

The best thing about the party was that there was not a single intelligence-related person present; nobody to spot or assess, develop or recruit, debrief or terminate, at least that I knew of, but who was I to judge. Krebs probably would have managed to get an intelligence report out of one of those models. Nobody from the Station showed up, even though I had invited them. Anyway, it wasn't a scene for khakis and deck shoes. The standard embassy-issue living room furniture, now draped in batik, came alive in its new location in the garden, which was lit with a thousand small lights high in the trees. The once banal yard looked as though it had been annexed and brought inside the old Dutch house, complete with the trees, the lights, the music, and the stars overhead. It was not a change in appearance, it was a total change in atmosphere.

The underlying sexuality and orgiastic mood was less subtle as the evening wore on and Ecstasy kicked in. A joint was handed around, and its smell combined with incense and the scent of oil lamps and wafted away into the branches overhead. Fortunately for the party, I had not chosen the music, or we would have needed other drugs. Instead, the smoothness of *Unchained Melody* inspired everyone into trancelike slow dances, and as I turned slowly with Agustina, I noticed the petting going on around me had become intimate—and hands were inside of shirts, legs wrapped around partners, breasts exposed.

It remained on that level, a gentle soft porn scene, with nothing going beyond a certain limit of dignity that everyone seemed to share. Still, all the positions of the Kama Sutra were acted out through the clothing out there, either while dancing on the lawn or lounging on the sofas, which were set up in various arrangements around the garden with suggestive candlelight giving each an atmosphere of its own. Couples sat with other couples, draping themselves comfortably so that any one of them could stroke the other three. They began to look like great, slender cats grooming one another gently, very gently, and getting smiles and gentle touches in return.

Dancing meant a slender catlike girl would slide her hand between my legs, then up my shirt, then away again. Occasionally, I tried the same with them, but they had a way in their hands that I lacked, a suppleness of attitude about what they were doing, as if to say this is just now—this dance, this moment, this drug, and tomorrow I will be unknown to you and you to me and neither of us will remember this.

The dream-like quality that permeated the garden was out of a past that Java carries like an old tune in its head, and that once in a while emerges from its spirit home. Java and night go hand in hand, with spirits living in trees and the sound of the Gamelan glonging out its amber, continuous non-melody, rising, falling, never stopping, the *Wayang* shadow puppet shows, lasting for entire nights until dawn and reenacting the Gita and the great battles between good and evil and the triumphs of Krishna and Arjuna. The spiritualism is piled so thickly on Java that it's hard for Islam to hold its place, and its application to a people so supple is often tenuous.

Things wound down as dawn approached, and Agustina and I curled up on a sofa in the garden. Couples slept into daylight, and in the morning the house was still full of people.

Saturday afternoon we all went up to the pool at the Hotel Borobudur and lounged like Europeans until dusk, drinking lemonade and punch under the great, shady trees and watching the French tan themselves. That night, we rented movies and watched *The Year of Living Dangerously*, the film in which Mel Gibson plays Guy Hamilton, an Aussie journalist covering the Indonesian revolution and the fall of Soekarno. The movie confirmed much of what I was feeling about Java, the old and the new, good spirits and malignant ones.

It was a short, easy week at work, and it slipped past with little to add to my situation. Not a word was said in the office about the party, and soon it was the end of the week. I felt I was moving softly toward something, but its face eluded me. I was happy in my home, where I felt like a *bapak*, the father of the house, with many family members always around.

The Agency had other ideas, however, and you heard it touted that one should leave a tour with no friends from that country. "We're not the Peace Corps." It made me a bit sad that we were not the Peace Corps, though, and I realized I wouldn't remain in CIA after this. I could easily stay in Indonesia with Agustina and just live.

I left the embassy early on Friday in a taxi instead of having my driver pick me up. When I got home, Mas, my driver, and Parto were standing by the car, my boards were on the roof, and the car was packed for the weekend. Agustina came out with a towel on her head, grinning, and we got in the car and went south.

This was her part of Java, the Sunda district, which has its own language, its own origins within the Hindu traditions, and strange tribes that live in isolation. The Badui people live in a remote mountain area of West Java, and their mysticism contributes to their mystery. Occasionally, we would see one dressed all in white "out among the English" on walkabout from their closed society. They worship Siliwangi, a Hindu god, and reject the Islam of Java.

We slid out of Jakarta on the old car's smooth shocks, my two staffers driving and riding shotgun, while Agustina and I unzipped each other in the back seat under a blanket, and watched the car rise onto the mountain. Eventually the great peak came into view, and soon we were on the downward slope, time measured by our playful sex, which the boys in the front had the good sense not to notice. When her head disappeared under the blanket, I feigned sleep and kept myself very still.

   Later we unwound ourselves and the ride got even more interesting as we passed the lush *sawah* (rice) fields and massive palms, ladies with breasts bared working in fields, and water buffalo being bathed in rivers next to the bridge.

   The scenery of Java was now so natural to me that it looked like home, but I knew I was seeing it through Agustina's eye, sharing in her familiarity with it in a way I could never do without a native's vision. She spoke the local language, and when we stopped alongside the road we wouldn't have a coke but a coconut. We were not foreigners but locals, interesting to our hosts, who could now bridge the gap between us through her.

   Eventually the road meandered to the sea, and we headed for a beach called Carita, where there was just a small wave, perfect for this weekend. We got a hotel room and let the two staffers fend for themselves.

   After resting, they returned for us. We piled in the car and went off to the surf. The few people who were on the beach when we arrived witnessed the great American who alighted from his ancient Peugeot as if it were a chariot, whilst his menservants carried his surfboard down to the edge of the water and began to wax it, as though they were his gunbearers. Agustina thought it was hilarious, and I sheepishly accepted the honor, but I did get some weird looks from the Aussie surfers in the water. Fortunately for me I took off and was immediately covered up by the tube. Then I was okay. Later, I finally got my two guys to take a board out, which they did together. They got knocked around quite a bit by the waves. Being tough fuckers though, they kept at it, and by late afternoon they were riding tandem.

They kept the distance between us clear, those guys. I was the boss with my lady, and they were there to serve. In the evening I gave them some cash and they probably went off and got laid or went gambling with local guys. It was easy for them to mingle; they were at home.

Agustina and I sat at a table on the sand eating shellfish, which was cooked in the restaurant and brought out to us on the beach. I drank too many Bintangs and it was an all round wonderful day.

Chapter Ten

On Sunday we walked on the beach, a family among families. The waves were very small as they usually were on this coast, which faces Sumatra and the volcano Krakatau. The swells from the Indian Ocean had to come around the Ujung Kulon nature preserve to get here. I felt like an old married fart now, with my girl and my two sherpas, and I wasn't planning on getting too radical.

    I had a beer at around nine a.m. and felt great about that being my breakfast. Then I went out and surfed it off, pushing Agustina into waves in the shallow water, as I walked along the coral with reef socks. She did pretty good—stood right up and even pulled a turn or two. After that we had a nap and prawns, checked out of the hotel and geared up for a nap on the ride back home.

    If one week had been easy, a tough one was always coming. Now, I had to come up with a plan to meet my Iraqi. I figured Biu would reappear in Jakarta on business or some other wealthy Brazilian activity, but I had no idea what kind of business that might be, nor how that business would be conducted, and it seemed a fair bet that my cover would wear thin unless I got my act together.

Another and altogether more serious problem faced me. When I had been considered the class dunce, Larry had left me alone. Now I had caught the Station's attention, causing a shift in the cosmos. I saw Larry looking at me on a couple of occasions, which I felt sure he had never done in the past, since that first night when he picked me up.

Some people are designed to be middle management, and it seems to suit them to the ground. They feel a part of something only when they are in the middle, having come up from the lower end and having no reason to believe they will ever see the top. The middle is home for many people in government jobs. In those jobs, you need no vision, no greatness, no passion, and generosity of spirit is seldom rewarded. There is also a curious strain of mind, which is constantly doing smaller, nastier things than the rest of us—insect authority, it has been called. How could so-and-so be thinking of doing something so petty, so unproductive, so wrong? And yet, there is so-and-so steaming full speed ahead on a narrow, nasty path . . . the Branch Chief path.

Up until now I had stayed out of his way and he had only grudgingly allowed me to have assignments at all. The only reason I was chosen for the Iraqi op was that JR pushed for it, and Larry wasn't going to take on JR. But now I was in the spotlight, and something had to be done. Larry stepped into the office where three of us sat at desks and jocularly said, "Hey Gus, can you come in for a minute please."

I gulped and went in. "So now that you are working on this Iraqi operation I'm taking you off the dip circuit so you won't blow your cover."

I had to confess he had a point. The Iraqi guy was a diplomat, and could show up at a cocktail party at any moment and see me there and know instantly that I was not really Biu from Braziu.

My banishment would set me back badly though in the race for meaningless recruitments and the resulting promotions, and we both knew that. If I couldn't meet foreign diplomats and host country bureaucrats in some kind of systematic way, I would never recruit anybody whose title made them sound important. The diplomatic circuit was the primary fishing ground, and I had just been kicked out. Meanwhile, I was sure we both felt the Iraqi operation would go nowhere, and I would end up with nothing. He had me, so I just agreed with him.

As I left, he called after me, "I've already cleared this with the Chief," as though he thought I might try to go over his head, but I just figured I was screwed, and had no plans to try to rectify the situation.

In a way, it would be a relief not to have to attend those stupid parties. There were never any interesting girls there, just a bunch of dowdy diplomatic types, and most of the parties didn't even serve alcohol, so no big loss. Eventually I would have to explain to someone what I did in Jakarta for two years, but by that time I would probably be ready to get out of this crap and do something interesting like draw cartoons or something, which I had once shown some slight promise in, or maybe that Peace Corps thing would work out, or the Wildlife Fund or Greenpeace. Anyway, I was going to be pretty much un-promotable.

My best approach now was to try to work this Iraqi deal and enjoy myself along the way. In fact, it was time to give the guy a call, so I prepared a scenario and sent it by memo to Larry and the front office. It was very carefully worded and had a strange sane scent to it, which I had mastered as the best way to get ideas across around here. It was accepted pretty much without question, although Larry did correct my grammar, or rather he changed my grammar to his grammar, before it went forward.

The plan called for me to phone Saleh at his home in the evening during the week and tell him I was in town and would like to get together on the weekend. We stayed away from Friday due to its significance as the holy day for Muslims, and shot for a Saturday night, which blew the whole weekend. I would check into a hotel in alias (per chapter five, CIA handbook, and merit badge guide) so that if he checked the record he would see that Bill Santos, a Brazilian, was registered, and I would be covered. I would have to spend Saturday night in the hotel as well, or at least go in and mess up the bed. I planned to do that all right, but first I would have to see how things went with Saleh.

After my plan was approved I went out to make the call but got nervous and put it off until the next day. On Thursday I couldn't wait any longer so I phoned him in the afternoon and found him at home. In my anxiety, I had forgotten how easy it was to talk to this guy. He was pretty nice and funny and was happy to get together on the weekend.

Back at the Station, Larry seemed to be looking for fault in what I had done, so I put on a hangdog pessimism about my likelihood of success, hoping to stay off the skyline that way. It kind of worked, but Larry wanted to remind me of the rules. After he finished I felt as though I had been warned about all the mistakes I was likely to make, which were far more mistakes than I had known were possible. It had been much easier talking to the enemy.

I was pretty nervous by the time the weekend came, so I sent Agustina to her mother's house in Bandung as a present, and to get her out of the way. She had been having some stomach cramps and wasn't likely to be much fun to look after, and besides I was on a big mission now, and feeling kind of self-important and authoritative. She went happily, and as usual caused me no problem or grief. On Friday night we went down to the Tanamur disco, all five or six of us guys who now used my house as a center.

The Tanamur is Jakarta's oldest discotheque and its clientele was universal, meaning anyone might be seen there. Its customers span the social spectrum from the very wealthy to the very needy, and everyone in between. One might see an ambassador or two in there; one would most certainly see a prostitute or two in there, and indeed one might be led to question any perceived differences between their jobs. It was set up with a cat walk and aside from the girls who danced up there, you might see Dutch oil executives, *banci* (she-male cross dressers), U.S. Marines, whatever. On this occasion the place enjoyed a visit from the Italian Navy, whose ship was in the port of Ancol.

The five of us were standing in the center of the dance floor when they came in—Italian sailors, striding in together shoulder abreast in their white uniforms and caps. They were an impressive sight—many were tall, tough looking blokes. They clearly planned to dominate the place that night, and to look after one another. When they made their majestic entrance, marching right down the middle of the place, everyone easily gave way to them, as though a parade were coming through. Everyone except Elvis that is, who, as a former Legionnaire, had a tradition to uphold, I suppose.

He stood his ground in the middle as they approached, as alone as Horatio at the Bridge, and I saw a look of concern cross the big lead sailor's face. Clearly they had anticipated the response they were getting from the rest of the place, which was to make a hole for them and get the fuck out of the way. But those Italian sailors didn't want any part of the Irishman, and broke their ranks around him.

There was just something about the guy, standing there, feet planted, hair pulled back in a kind of girly-looking pony tail, chin jutting out like a cartoon. He was something out of another age.

We all took girls home from the bar than night, and it was not quiet in the least. Elvis had a tradition of sending home photos of girls with their knickers down, somehow or another displaying a small flag from his rugby club, which he would plant on any convenient flagpole. On this occasion he tried to use a slender bottle from the kitchen cabinet for a flagpole, and a young lady's anus as its base. Unfortunately for both of them, the cap leaked. More unfortunately still, the slim bottle he had selected for a flagpole had contained Sambal, Indonesian hot sauce. A lot of shrieking and cursing of Elvis and of men of Ireland ensued, followed by the sound of showering and forgiveness before silence reigned once more . . . or nearly reigned. The last thing I heard was Stretch shouting from the living room (to which he had been banished), "That really burns my ass, yes it does. Really burns my ass."

By Saturday morning all was well. The sun rose upon a tranquil world, the girls were gone, and Elvis was much chastened. I had to psyche up for my meeting, which by now was really scaring the crap out of me. I just didn't know what to expect, and I viewed my brief rapport with Saleh on the airplane as totally irrelevant and unhelpful. I felt it would really be much better if I were meeting the guy for the first time.

The idea of actually recruiting an Iraqi seemed outlandish to me. It was a pretend thing, a fiction, and nobody really expected it to happen. Relations between the countries were quickly giving rise to rumors of war, and there was no target more important to the CIA in Indonesia. Iraqis were comfortable in Indonesia, as their Islam relates, and they meet a better class of hooker through their religion, as the Turks and Egyptians also did. It was a great advantage, and got you into all kinds of small doors not open to other nationalities and religions. On the other hand you had the fasting, no drinking, and prayer at all hours. On the even other hand, you could have a harem, so I guessed it evened out overall.

As evening approached, I took three taxis to Ancol, checked into the hotel and waited. Saleh called at eight p.m. to confirm that I was there, and arrived around nine. We had a drink in the lobby. I had already hatched a plan to introduce the American angle.

"So you are a Brazilian," he stated, as though he knew otherwise.

"I grew up in Rio de Janeiro and studied in United States," I told him, in perfect Brazilian English.

"Which university?"

"UCLA, in Los Angeles; it has good department for business."

"Oh," he said, "That's a wonderful university. You watch *Baywatch*?"

"Of course, we call *Buttwatch*, we love this movie in Braziu."

I wasn't sure how thick to lay on the accent, and I was kind of finding my way. I was so fucking nervous that I kept on talking even with nothing to add to the conversation. We ordered drinks and I settled down a bit. He drank whiskey, straight, and I had a beer. This wasn't so bad. Then we moved to a Chinese restaurant nearby and talked over dinner about Brazil and girls, which I thought would be the big common ground. He was interested in the girls, especially Brazilian girls, whose dark strong bodies he had seen in films of Carnaval.

Thankfully I had my shit together on Brazil, and we talked about the Afro Brazilian elements of culture, the Samba schools, Carnaval, the Orixas and the pantheon of deities imported from Africa, Candomble, the black magic from Bahia, Capoeira, the martial art that came from slaves disguising their training as dance, and so on. It was pretty clear I was either partly or wholly Brazilian. When I was done with my soliloquy I heaved a big sigh and relaxed. He asked me what else we do in Brazil for fun. Before I could stop myself I said, "We go surfing."

"I love to see this sport!" he said. "They are surfing here in Indonesia also, and I would like to learn this." Before I knew it I had let him believe that I would be setting him up to go surfing and we would go the next time I came to town. It was done and there was no undoing it. I felt that if this relationship were to succeed at all, I would have to make good on my promise to take this guy surfing. The guy himself was no problem. We got along great, but Larry had told me to strictly insulate my personal life from this operation, and that I would be in trouble if I didn't follow his instructions, and, blah, blah, blah. I was already in trouble when Larry took me off the dip circuit. How much more trouble did he think I could get into?

We wound up the evening with a drive around town in his car. There I was, speaking with an accent that was beginning to slur slightly from the Bintangs I had drunk, in an Iraqi car

Surfing the C.I.A.

with diplomatic tags, tooling around Jakarta pretending I didn't know my way round. I got a scare when he pulled up in front of the Iraqi Embassy, which was directly in front of a stop sign, and I heard his turn indicator go on. I was talking faster than ever, wondering what I would do if he turned into the compound. Should I roll out of the car and hightail it? Larry would pull out his rule book and write me up for sure, and that would be the end of my career.

We sat at the stop sign for a long moment, then finally moved forward and turned onto a side street away from the Iraqi compound. I kept on talking but I just about shit. My main concern was to keep him away from Blok M, because we were clearly looking for a place to flirt with some trashy girls, and the Tambora was a well-known end-up bar. Fortunately he knew a place in Kuningan, and we went there.

The non-Western bars were very different from those the Americans and Aussies frequented. They were darker and quieter with different music, more Indonesian. There were girls in the place, and we chatted and had another beer, and both of us got a bit potted. Then it was full-on surf talk. I told him about surf spots I had chalked up over the years, which was a pretty good list even before Indo. He had been to Spain, and I had surfed Mundaka, a fast big left on the Basque coast. This also gave me a chance to rattle off some Spanish, which impressed him no end. We went to the bar at the Mandarin on Jalan Sudirman for one more beer. We were both now somewhat wasted and laughing and kind of incoherent.

I was glad I had chosen my Brazilian disguise as it allowed me a natural, casual, rich guy way of dress. Inside we were approached by two *bancis* who looked very beautiful until you noticed something wrong about them. We got a lot of laughs over that.

Everything was fine until Snake Woman appeared in the doorway. I thought I was dead, but she said hello and kept on walking, obviously on some wicked commercial mission of her own. Saleh watched her go.

I made sure this was our last beer, "Saidera," as we say in Brazil, and got us the fuck out of there, suddenly feeling sober. We drove and talked some more, and he mentioned Blok M, but I managed to steer him back to Ancol. At this point both of us were pretty drunk, and we went past the park at Ancol where the girls stand around and come over to your car. This was the old sleaze pit of North Jakarta, which, along with the cemetery, served as a brothel in Soekarno's time. Finally, he dropped me back at the hotel, and I made plans to meet him in two weeks for a weekend at the beach.

At the hotel I relaxed, smoked a Cuban cigar and phoned the desk to request massage service to my room.

"Namanya siapa Meester?" the girl asked me, helping me get undressed.

"Nama saya Biu, Mbak," I told her, "Biu, dari Braziu."

Chapter Eleven

With the second meeting a success, my stock went up in the Station and down with Larry. I tried to avoid him but I was constantly screwing up cables. My grammar and syntax had been okay until I got to Jakarta, when it apparently began a serious and steady decline. Basically Larry was watching me like an eagle spotting for trout, and I was bound to do something wrong before too long, that being my nature.

I had a stack of books next to my desk, and I noticed they had been moved slightly—one of those things you wouldn't think about in a less hostile environment, but you notice otherwise. Beyond doubt, someone had been looking at those books, or more likely at the covers of those books. That was a dismal thought. First, it indicated I was being studied even closer than I thought, and second, it meant that some of my dirty little secrets were found out. I felt as if I had stuffed my soiled underpants behind the dresser and they had been discovered by the maid.

Until now, Bukowski had been tucked discreetly under Hemingway's *Short Stories*. Hemingway was acceptable, although there was an atmosphere in the office that indicated a coolness toward readers in general. Now, Bukowski was sticking out slightly. I would never be so careless. Someone had obviously moved these books. *Tropic of Cancer* was under that, also shifted from its original posture. Under those, and out of order, were *The Dharma Bums* and a book of poems by Gary Snyder. "Shit, I'm screwed," I thought.

But the calamity was unavoidable, and there were important projects to pursue. Someone in our group—I think it was one of the Aussies—discovered that Harley Davidson had manufactured motorcycles in Indonesia for a number of years before the revolution, maybe up through the early sixties, and there was a guy in East Jakarta with a shop full of classic bikes. In order to stay abreast of the latest fashion in our crowd, I would have to figure out a way to acquire one of these bikes.

At the shop, not only were there Harleys, with their "suicide shifters" and wartime paint jobs, but also some old BMWs and a number of English bikes. I fell in love with a 1951 BSA 650 twin cylinder beauty, which was rebuilt and running. I figured it would greatly enhance my social standing, which was already good, especially since the party.

To get this important status symbol, I would have to engage in some creative financing. I was overdrawn and living on credit from the embassy commissary, and picking up what meals I could with change on my counter-surveillance runs. My solution was to bite the bullet and join the American Club, the chief advantage of which was that I could charge meals there. Membership was free for embassy personnel, and on Sunday nights they had Mongolian barbecue. That was all that mattered. It also had a pool and tennis courts, but the membership roster included the last people I wanted to see on the weekend. It was helpful for Elvis though, whose tastes ran more toward Western women; after I joined the club he quickly acquired a standing among the membership, in particular among the embassy wives.

Membership in the club allowed me to invest nearly my entire paycheck in my upward mobility and soon the English bike was sitting in our driveway, leaking oil. It would run just long enough to get around the neighborhood, and usually crap out just as the rider reached maximum distance from home. It was excellent for scaring the old Javanese *ibu* ladies walking down the sidewalks with bundles on their heads.

Kamal, of course, bought a Harley, being a good Turk, and soon there was an assemblage of motorcycles and riders trading off bikes, jackets and other gear in the driveway of the old Dutch house as though it were a Café-Racing club. Rides were limited to my neighborhood of Kebayoran for the most part, as Jakarta traffic is horrendous on the main roads, but more ambitious plans were always being laid for trips across Java and for other objectives just within the realm of possibility; but not much really happened.

Two other projects quickly distracted my attention from my bike. In fact, the bike quickly became a vehicle primarily used by Parto to run errands, and by Stretch to court Snake Woman, who looked very much at home sitting on a bike, and was frequently photographed departing from that house. She was photographed more departing than arriving, being a very photogenic kind of girl from behind.

The first big idea to loom up was the challenge of climbing Gunung Gede, the Sundanese mountain, which looms up near Bandung in West Java, just outside Jakarta. The spark for this idea came from Stretch. Stretch had intended to be a mountaineer when he left the outback, and was headed for Nepal when the opportunity had arisen for him to become a garbage collector in Jakarta, and this interesting career offer interrupted his plans. Stretch had arrived in Indo with a book called *Trekking in Nepal*, which he intended to read as he worked his way across Southeast Asia toward the Himalayas. But that was before he got his big break in the sanitation field.

We learned from the book that climbing would require cold weather gear, and so the mountain would have to be climbed at night. This reasoning was never closely scrutinized, but nonetheless it carried the day. The other project was a country car, which came to us through divine intervention, when the neighbor gave us an old Toyota Land Cruiser in exchange for commissary privileges. It meant I would have to take orders from him for American products available only at the commissary, such as TV dinners and cereal, not to mention booze, but I would have my gunbearers do all the heavy labor, and I would simply endure the annoyance of being in his indenture with stoicism and with the knowledge that I was now a two-car family.

The jeep would need some work, and we pooled money to hire a team of guys that somebody knew. They immediately moved into our garage, set up a welding plant, and went over the body of the car gutting the rusted spots, which didn't leave a lot of car. Then they went to work on the engine.

When the Land Cruiser finally was ready, it looked like something off Fantasy Island. It was a ragtop buggy with two layers of waterproof canvas stretched from the roll bar to the windshield. The surfboards would be carried on a built-in rack, which strapped them down at the front and rear. The rear portion of the surfboard rack allowed boards to be locked onto the car, which would at least confuse a thief, if not frustrate him completely into leaving the thing alone. The guys had replaced the doors and windows, so it couldn't rain in, much. The suspension was stiffer than the old Peugeot's, and the heavy duty shocks would be able to work through ruts and sand. It had bucket seats, a rear passenger seat far less ample than the Peugeot's had (so much for blow jobs on the way to the beach), and a steel box welded in behind the back seat to hold surfing equipment, beer and other essential items. In order to be totally clandestine, the buggy was painted bright red.

Initial test rides were taken to downtown Jakarta, where the vehicle performed well in traffic and was shown capable of jumping a sidewalk curb. Stretch drove it across the flowerbeds and nearly into the fountain in the circle in front of the Hotel Indonesia where the statue of Donny and Marie Osmond stands. It would have been impounded except for the diplomatic license tags. After this event, we decided to register it locally to stay out of trouble. We figured if the car ever got impounded, it would be better off not reflecting back on the U.S. Embassy, so we put it in Parto's name.

The first mission of the new vehicle was to transport the ascent team, consisting of Gus, Elvis, Kamal and Stretch, to base camp at Gunung Gede, which we did in early evening, arriving at the road head at nightfall. We were prepared with down vests, hiking boots, and rucksacks containing sandwiches and beer. From the road head, it was an easy start on a clear path through the Cibodas Garden Park at the foot of the mountain, and for a while, the whole thing looked too easy. But the Gunung sits 2,958 meters above sea level and it would be about ten kilometers up the path, which was overgrown with fallen branches and other obstacles easily negotiated in daylight. At night, however, they worked like an obstacle course, leaving us bruised and scratched by branches and stones. Everyone had at least a couple of tumbles, and Kamal nearly fell off the mountain.

The plodding gait set by Elvis would have been more apt to his mountain regiment in the craggy peaks of Corsica. He moved out into the lead and we could hear him shouting back to us, spanking us along with French war whoops and other vulgarities. Stretch seemed to move his lanky frame easily, if a little lazily, and kept his own pace, which outdistanced me

Surfing the C.I.A.

considerably. I was still a fit surfer, but the muscles used in ascending mountains bear no relation to those used descending waves; I had to admit to near exhaustion soon after my second hour of walking. Kamal brought up the rear like the overweight diplomat he was, and could be heard cursing and wheezing a ways behind. Thus we continued toward Valhalla for several hours, just within earshot of all the others, and just beyond the range where a conversation could exist, our party spread evenly with all accounted for.

As I marched, my thoughts went back to the eight months I spent goofing off at The Farm. As part of our CIA training, the class of men and women donned camouflage gear and field-stripped assault rifles, went on patrols and met for sexual encounters in the woods. The main experience of The Farm had been the laughs and the friendships that emerged. Never having been much of a military type, I had guessed my way through the exercises, and nearly broke my neck by falling into a pit while on patrol. I was nothing to be proud of as a paramilitary type, and made it through the course by befriending the instructors and convincing them that I had other skills. They let me slide on through, even after I got lost on the land navigation course and ended up on a college campus nearby. I guess I never would have made a good Marine.

Halfway up, we broke for an hour in a trailside hut. One of the ascent team produced a joint, and it began to make the rounds. When it got to me, I balked. I hadn't been high since before joining the Agency, having only received secondary marijuana smoke at the party, which works quite well by the way, and I had thus far managed to obey the Agency's strict ban on marijuana smoking. But it was too much to bear to be halfway up a mountain in Indonesia after midnight and refuse a joint, so I proceeded to break another rule and got very stoned in the thin air, with the exertion of my ascent providing an assist.

Elvis, of course, was only slightly winded by the time we reached the top, but the rest of us could barely open a beer, which we managed notwithstanding. That achievement complicated the descent considerably. I never did see the great view from the summit, since we had neglected to check the weather report and the top third of the mountain had been clouded over for weeks. How were we to know that? We got there at night.

The mountain climb, though not very scenic and altogether a tiresome experience, was nonetheless the closing of a circle around the four of us. It was a crucible from which a cabal, a sacred brotherhood was emerging, through the irony of circumstance. The winds reached our ears carrying a rumor of war, and, like pirates, we prepared for our own destinies by breaking with our monarchs. I felt an affection for my brothers of the mountain, and even after the pot wore off and we were down at base camp finishing up the beers, I felt a glow of warmth and gratitude for these friends, now trading insults and laughing at one another's battle scars.

Kamal had torn his camouflage trousers on a tree stump, and his shin was bloodied. I was covered in bruises and scratched where I was not bruised. Stretch was little the worse for wear, having spent ten years in the outback, and Elvis was fresh as a daisy.

The drive back to Jakarta was one of those quiet ones that adventurers know, where the experience looms behind you and other matters seem inconsequential. Like the effect of a mantra repeated, the exhausting stimulation of a great experience clears the mind and brings life into focus. So, for me at least, daydreaming about the climb, too tired to make comments that came to mind, the ride was pregnant with exuberance and tempered by fatigue.

The feeling lasted until the traffic of Jakarta began. When that happened a bit of youth, a tiny bit of innocence was lost, and war came ever nearer.

Chapter Twelve

With the little boat of our band of pirates launched upon the shining sea, I went back to the embassy and bumbled around the office for the next week trying to look busy and up to my tasks. I had to sit through several wettings down at the hand of Larry. I even had my Walk-Man confiscated after wearing it at my desk. This was now worse than high school. I tried to think of other ways I might make a living, but none of them would get me to where I already was, and I was not so drawn to causes like the environment, world peace or animal rights that I was willing to sacrifice the proximity of righteous waves for the inner fulfillment of serving a good cause. Basically, I would have to shut up, and whatever shit was served up, I would have to take it like a rat. This of course gave me more reason to spend my evenings in Blok M and just enough justification to break the no-pot-smoking rule some more.

Meanwhile, something else was coming into focus in the Station. It was time for me to contact my Iraqi again, and that had me pretty nervous. I hadn't stated in my contact report that I planned to meet him at the beach, nor had I mentioned it to anyone in the Station, thinking it was better to give myself some time to think this over. Just as I was preparing to announce this and thinking it would be well received, I learned that Larry had cut in on my operation.

I had never seen this coming. I was not a seasoned enough bureaucratic gladiator to know the inner workings of these things, nor how to read the signs, so I was blind-sided. It seems that Larry had presented the Station Chief with a plan for himself and Krebs to have a chance encounter with two Iraqis, one of them being Saleh. The plan was made possible by Krebs, which I thought was typical, and Larry was just riding in as a parasite.

Krebs, whose primary defect in my mind was merely a lack of imagination and who really didn't have a mean streak to him, had learned that one of the other Iraqi diplomats frequented a certain club. He went to the club cast as a Canadian businessman and ran into two Iraqis, one of them being my guy.

Krebs told Larry, assuming Larry would send me in, but instead Larry contacted the Chief of Station at home to get approval, and then Larry and Krebs went back the next night and met the Iraqis. They had presented the Chief with a plan to double-team the two targets, which Larry had authored and cut himself in on, and they had the meeting the day before he told me I was out. They already had another meeting set up, with them posing as Canadians looking to buy oil from Iraq.

This took precedence over my meetings with Saleh. Larry, twisting the knife, told me he had already cleared this with the Chief. He told me I could now stand-down on any further meetings, so as not to cross wires with them. I thought it was a cheap trick, but he did make one good point: the fact that Krebs and Larry both had contacts gave them advantages over my operation. Also their experience would be more likely to yield success. So my great operation was shut down.

My initial reaction to this development was to be mildly disappointed that I was no longer a hero in the Station. My role hadn't lasted very long, and the immediate change in my reception said something about the fleeting nature of fortune. Yet I also felt a great sense of relief and safety in the knowledge that I was no longer responsible for something very important and closely watched.

Larry said nothing to me about perhaps putting me back on the diplomatic circuit or coming up with other targets for recruitment so that I would not be wasting my time here. The matter seemed to be closed. Some days I wished I had the whole thing back, but there were other matters to tend to, so that is where my effort went, right into my life outside the Station and outside of the American community.

Since I had made plans to go to the beach over the weekend, we made it into a surf safari, old California style, and on Friday three loaded surf wagons departed from the old Dutch house in Kebayoran. I drove the "new" Land Cruiser, with Agustina riding shotgun and Stretch in the back on the bench. Kamal drove his jeep, with Elvis and a couple of hookers who traveled, and Phil and Nick drove their *vehiculus magnus*. Beers were carefully stood up in coolers, ice was cascaded upon them, boards were placed in racks, and a five-foot barbecue grill we had ordered from the car guys was hoisted up and strapped on Kamal's roof. I dropped in a Beach Boys tape, and the action moved south across Java.

We arrived at Buana Ayu, our regular hotel, and Agustina and I got a room right away, one with a patio overlooking the little break right out front. Kamal got the same room we had shared before—the one with the curtain—and selected a girl from the back seat. Stretch and Elvis got a room with the remaining girl, who didn't seem concerned about the arrangement. Thus ensconced, we gorged on shrimp and Bintangs and retired early to my patio, where plans were made and marijuana smoked.

As eggy beer and cannabis swirled together within us, a curious truth serum resulted, at least among the brotherhood, who wanted to hear me say I was CIA. "How're you spelling that?" I shouted back, that being confirmation enough.

"Leave Gus alone! He's bugged!" Elvis howled, choking with laughter.

"The CIA are coming!" gurgled Stretch through a giggle.

Just then Kamal's pistol fell out of his boot, which was up on the table, and as the weapon hit the ground with a clump, a general chaos of laughter erupted. When it eventually subsided, it had brought the girls to the table along with a waiter, who was immediately barraged with absurd demands and slunk away puzzled.

Kamal said, "Anyway Gus, you American Spy, we have discussed it, and you can count on us." It was stated with sincerity, although the Turk was still snickering, but I unfortunately still had the giggles.

"How are you spelling U.S.?" was all I could manage. But I had a feeling then that I would be taking them up on the offer.

Saturday came clear and windless, with a small swell running from a direction that didn't work out front too well, although I did take Agustina out for a few early waves, just to get ourselves wet, as we say. We did an early surf check of Cimaja, the hard breaking reef across the rice padis, but the most excitement we found there was a *krait*, a poisonous snake basking itself on one of the ledges that served as a path through the *sawah*. Elvis was in the lead through the *sawah*, and, being the snake expert from his military training, stepped over it and shouted back to us not to step on it "because it'll kill you." This was immensely helpful information.

The surf was small and coming in at a strange angle, which did not work with Cimaja, and the tide was a bit too high. We opted for the Samudra Beach hotel, with its all-day food and drink service on the beach, and the powerful undertow beyond. We figured these would compensate for the smallness of the waves. When we got there it was breaking waist high, about thirty yards out, and looking like perfect girlfriend surf.

Surfing the C.I.A.

Setting up was a chore. I missed having my gun bearers to carry my board down to the water and wax it up—amazing how easy that was to get used to. When we finally got arranged, the girls had places to sit and read their magazines and our boards were standing up in the sand a-la-Waikiki, for maximum style effect. Then we lay down with a cold beer to study the menu.

The morning was warm and sunny, and with an early beer in me I was turning reflective. I looked over at my girl, who was now lying face down on her beach towel with her bikini top undone in the back, her well-formed body deepening its natural amber hue. I looked back at the hotel and the mountains behind it, their voluptuous green dripping down to the sea and out to the sea itself, deep blue and sunlit. I was mellow to the vomitus stage, and I wanted to remain in this blissful state among my friends at the beach forever. My career faded into nothing in the clear pre-noon sunshine, and I felt the need to get into motion and surf.

I stood up and selected my nine foot Hobie, and, after waxing her down myself, stroked smoothly into the lineup. I was swinging my board around and paddling into a three-foot wave, when I heard a familiar sound; "Biu! Biu my friend, how are you?"

Chapter Thirteen

Upon seeing Saleh, I executed the most complete wipeout possible on a wave this small, landing on my head on my board. I quickly tried to assemble a sense of place and juxtaposition, importing and exporting myself from numerous scenarios as I paddled toward him grinning. By the time I reached him I was Brazilian again.

The reunion was a happy one. We were both genuinely glad to see one another. There was nothing strange or out of character about meeting up at the beach. In fact now that the operation had been called off, I was feeling downright easy about the whole thing. My only problem would be that the group on the beach knew me as Gus the American diplomat. I was desperately thinking ahead as to how I would navigate through this one.

Saleh had been disappointed that I didn't phone him during the week, and had decided to come down to the beach anyway, with a young lady he knew from Jakarta. He had checked into the Samudra Beach Hotel, and had been reading in his Indonesia Handbook about the spirit of the Queen of the South Seas, N'yai Loro Kidul, who comes up from the sea and devours people. He had been wearing green trunks and had thrown them away when he learned the legend that anyone who wears green will be taken to the depths. He did a surface flip to show me his new trunks. With a Hawaiian floral pattern and drawstring, they looked like they were purchased from an ad in *Surfer* magazine.

We were both getting a kick out of his trunks when a nice set of waves loomed up outside. He quickly accepted the invitation to try the board, so I slipped my foot leash off and passed it over to him. There was no time for him to tie it on though, so I just pushed him shoreward as the first wave came through. He struggled to his knees, and rode the wave. Close in to shore, he managed to get to his feet for a few moments before I saw his Hawaiian trunks go end over boomkin as he wiped out in the shorebreak. Like a typical surfer, he was grinning as he paddled back out.

Before he reached me, Elvis was out on another board, and I could see Kamal and Stretch getting ready to come out. As Elvis paddled over, I said to him, "Don't ask anything, but this guy knows me as Bill, and I'm from Brazil."

"I knew you were a fucking spook, Gus. Whatever you say then." I recalled that Elvis was a soldier.

"Pass the word, mate!" I called to him. By this time Elvis was riding a wave and grinning at our new friend, who was getting smacked by the whitewater as he paddled out through wave after wave. I bodysurfed past him and alerted everyone on shore to the situation. I heard "Gus is Biu!" go around our group. Nobody asked questions, they just went right along with the plan, and from then on I was Biu, or for Stretch, Beu, which is Biu in Australian.

The only fly in the ointment was that the young lady who had accompanied Saleh from Jakarta turned out to be Snake Woman. She was sitting on the beach nearby. I couldn't see how I had missed her. This annoyed Stretch, but his heart was elastic, hence his nickname, and he soon accommodated these new arrangements in his fortune, much in the way he had sublimated the exchange of the Annapurna range for the garbage truck route in Jakarta.

Snake Woman had to be bribed, so we let Stretch execute this task, which raised him greatly in her esteem and gave him hope for the future. After this was done, Saleh came in, awkwardly carrying the big board, his Hawaiian trunks glistening in the daylight, and Snake Woman brought their towels over to our group.

Saleh was the center of attention as the group reassembled and compared wave and wipeout stories. He was laughing and grinning and joking, and everyone was having a good time. I began to notice, however, that Saleh was avoiding questions about where he was from. Once I perceived this I was sympathetic to the problem, having the same one myself. In a quiet moment he took me aside discreetly and confessed his dilemma.

"Biu, I think better to say I am from the Lebanon to your friends."

"I understand," I told him, "but these are not my friends, they are also your friends."

"Thank you. Still maybe better to say I am from the Lebanon."

"No worries, Dude," I assured him, and a pact was sealed between us.

"By the way," I added in the event someone should slip, "my second name is Gustavo. Sometimes people call me like that."

"No worries, Dood," he said, trilling his r's. I decided he was not quite ready for Malibu.

The surf improved, and Saleh was a pretty good gremmie. He caught a lot of waves over the course of the afternoon, but the greatest performance by far was from Snake Woman, whose bikini already was attracting attention on the beach. When she got on the board, it was clear that her talents were wasted on whoring, and she could have mastered surfing if she spent less time on her back. Even her paddling looked proficient right from the start, and that was only the beginning. Saleh pushed her into the first wave, and after that she paddled into them herself. She took her share of wipeouts, raising spectators to their feet each time she fell in hopes she would lose her bikini, but, by mid-afternoon she was consistently standing and riding. She even executed a few turns before evening. Then she and Saleh went tandem, much to the dismay of Stretch, who was forced to witness the spectacle.

Snaky balanced the board and took his hands on her hips, and she guided them into Samudra surfing stardom. Even the tourists took notice of their act. People were applauding when the pair arrived upon the beach.

Finally we broke camp, and agreed to reassemble down the beach for a luau in the evening. Back at the Buana Ayu, I was at a loss as to how to explain to my friends about Saleh, but I needn't have worried. Nobody seemed to care where the guy was from, as he was nice and funny and seemed to be a decent guy. Stretch couldn't get over Snake Woman running off with the Arab guy, but he wasn't in earnest. Stretch told us that he himself had been "engaged" for twelve years back in Australia, and his way of viewing women had an impermanence, which was confirmed by these events. In short, he got over it like a man, and was friendly as ever to everyone.

After a rest and a shower, we set up the luau in front of the Pasar Monyet in our usual position on the beach, with the buggies right out on the sand, coolers sitting on the tailgates, and the Beach Boys startling the birds and the monkeys in the trees in the parking lot. We gathered driftwood, dug a pit, then placed the barbecue grill over part of it so that there was a campfire and a cooking fire, separate but connected.

Saleh arrived at dusk with Snake Woman who was looking fine and tropical, moving up in the world. I could see her gliding through cocktail parties on the dip circuit, all trace of sleaze behind her, but still flirtatious enough to promote a husband's, or even her own, career. An Indonesian Eva Peron. Saleh obviously had been back to the store where he bought his trunks, and now was dressed in similar jams that reached his ankles, sandals and a T-shirt. With his short cropped hair and mustache, he looked like an early California surfer with Mexican blood. He hesitated only slightly and accepted an ice cold Bintang, and we sang along to the Beach Boys and danced on the beach while the frozen steaks sizzled on the grill. We did them Brazilian style, with only rock-salt pounded into them as seasoning, and sliced them on a board that was passed around to pick from.

Saleh seemed to enjoy the Brazilian touch, yet didn't question as my accent faded over the course of the evening.

As we all talked, I began to realize how little connected I was to the embassy community. My connection was so tenuous it was not even necessary to camouflage it for Saleh's sake. The subject simply didn't come up. We talked as though the Dutch house belonged to Stretch, which to all appearances, it did. The mellowness I had felt during the day was restored, and I felt at ease with my friends (and, of course, my enemy), watching the campfire, stealing glances at Snake Woman's curves whenever they presented an elegant angle, but unwilling to trade my amiable and forgiving partner for a look under Snaky's sarong.

Saleh accepted the joint that was inevitably produced, and got as stoned as the rest of us. No one asked whether he had smoked before. It didn't seem natural to do so. What did seem natural was the way he took it, partook of it, and passed it on, just like something out of Kerouac, and this thought got me moving in my own direction.

I eventually insinuated my own music onto the car stereo, and watched as the group slowly aroused itself from its after-dinner stupor to dance around the campfire like a bunch of wild Indians as the sound of the Grateful Dead wafted out over the sands by the Indian Ocean. I stepped back to piss by the trees, and the scene I looked back upon was one of woodland nymphs and mummers doing rites around a campfire, springing up and down, backlit by firelight on the sand.

At length the embers began to glow and the energy level of the mummers to wane. We sat around the fire in a semi-circle facing the sea and spoke of nothing and everything. Stretch told about the sheep station down in Australia, riding jeeps and motorbikes out on the range, staying out for months at a time, and showed how he had nearly lost his foot in a motorbike crash. He explained how it was natural to be on the dole until a certain age down there, and then you should make up your mind to work and get out of the city, which is what he had done.

Elvis spoke of his travels with the pirates and his adventure on a mountain in East Java, when the lightning struck a rock just yards away.

I spoke of Bahia, the old colonial capital of Brazil, and of its proximity to Africa, and the culture that resulted, and of events I had seen there. Snake Woman talked about London, and her voice had a new softness. Saleh said little, but listened and smiled and poked the fire with a stick. Nobody mentioned the war.

Chapter Fourteen

Sunday morning we woke up on the beach, had a swim, and broke camp. Everyone was a bit groggy from beer, pot and sand for a bed. Blankets and sleeping bags were scattered all around and the campfire area was a bullring scene of dead bottles and smoldering remains of the fire, pieces of charred meat still left on the grill, and assorted flotsam and jetsam, including some underclothing I recognized as belonging to Snake Woman. It seemed a shame to have paid for a hotel, but we would still have a shower and a rest before heading home. Saleh and Snaky went their way, and I promised to give him a call during the week if I came to town.

My disguise seemed increasingly thin, but it held. I had been imprecise about my residential arrangements, muttering about Singapore occasionally, but Saleh had not pursued the subject, and, in turn, had muttered about Beirut. It was a symmetrical convenience that each of us had a dirty secret to preserve, and we seemed to have entered into a tacit agreement to support one another's pretense.

On the ride home I had enough to ponder, such as whether I should even report this contact or not. Should it be a grand finale to the operation, where I submit that Larry was really the lead officer approaching this Iraqi diplomat? This would avert Larry's wrath, but would it not also cause more problems for me? On the other hand I could keep mum about it, but where was that going to lead? Could I pretend not to have met him and get away with it? I finally came down on this side, since I already had plenty of stuff I wasn't reporting.

During the week I was forced to sit through Larry telling the entire staff about his progress with the Iraqi target. He was now both developing his own target for recruitment and also supervising Krebs and providing him with helpful operational advice. It appeared reasonable to believe that both operations would be successful and result in recruitments of Iraqis, who would then provide insight into Saddam Hussein and the Iraqi regime's intentions regarding Kuwait.

The fact that I had actually done something against the Iraqis was entirely forgotten, but I resolved to hold my tongue, partly out of spite and partly out of an uneasiness about crossing swords with middle management. Larry even got an extra jab in by stating, at the conclusion of his presentation, that he believed the chances of success were nearly one hundred percent, "now that we have our best officers on this." That was the fucking end. There was no reason to reiterate the fact that

I was the worst officer in the Station. I just put the whole thing out of my head.

Later on that day, after the staff meeting was concluded and everyone went back to their desks jabbering about Larry and Krebs and their great operation, I noticed one of my cables had gone through Larry with no editing whatsoever. I wondered what accounted for the sudden improvement in my grammar and syntax.

Christmas was coming, and that meant some time off, and obviously, surfing. Lots of Americans were going back home for the holidays, but I would stay out here and catch some waves, and that was exactly what my parents expected me to do. My sister would be home from college with them, and I would phone on Christmas day.

I understood the bars in Jakarta would be closed on Christmas day, but other than that, Christmas was just one of a number of religious holidays sanctioned by a government that accepted all major religions except Judaism. The question was where to surf. I opted to stay in West Java, close to home, as it would get fewer vacationing surfers than Nias, Grajagan, or Bali, and therefore would be much less crowded. Also I had been wanting to do a drive into some backcountry, and West Java was still fairly wild. There were said to be elephants, tigers, and the mysterious Javanese Rhinoceros out there in the bush, and I half expected to come upon some of these beasts.

The only traveling companion I could muster was Parto, and he did it out of a general good nature and probably to spend some time away from his wife. When the day came, I left the house in the care of Stretch and the other brigands, and lit out with Parto driving. I was dressed as a cross between Douglas McArthur and Jimmy Hendrix, armed with my BB gun and pipe.

The route took us south, through known territory, to Pelabuhan Ratu. We then went west along the coast highway, up and down mountains, through verdant rice padis and palm forests, and finally, into the jungle. This was not a surf trip, and I didn't even bring my board. I knew I could count on Parto to drive all night, so I brought something else instead—one of the dozen hits of LSD that my California pal Dale Sweeney had sent me as a micro-dot in a letter.

When I'd opened the letter and seen the acid, I had nearly chucked it, but that was before I realized that I wasn't long for CIA and while I was trying to obey all the rules. Fortunately my deepest instincts had instructed me to put it into a drawer with all my other mail and hold on to it. I had cut it into mild doses, and as we departed Pelabuhan, I put one onto my tongue. The familiar taste corrupted my saliva with hallucinogen.

Parto was the best companion for such a journey, as my sworn protector and servant, and would provide an insulation from the wild and wooly world. I had lain in a selection of music, mostly old acid rock that was designed to last through the six or eight hours of the trip, beginning with Jefferson Airplane and Jim Morrison, and moving through some lighter stuff like we heard in Bali, U2 and Gypsy Kings, and then finally getting hardcore with my beloved Grateful Dead.

Surfing the C.I.A.

The area of operation would be the car and an area of about fifteen feet around the car whenever it stopped; I would be safe within those parameters. This was all rehearsed by me, a veteran tripper with a pretty good idea of how the thing would go.

I was drinking a beer when the liftoff came, and for the next six hours I was commanding the jeep forward into the night with an extension of my will. The joy became tangible and thought merged with light and sound with depth. It was Java that ran through me on the ride, and I was Semar, the Javanese clown of the *Wayang*, who serves as a comic leader and foil for other characters of the pantheon of Javanese and Sanskrit gods.

As we entered a village, Parto would stop and present our *surat jalan*, which allowed me free passage through the region. I would pay my respects to the headman of the village, and we would proceed. At one village in a particularly remote forest spot next to the sea on the southern coast, the entire town was watching a *Wayang* shadow puppet performance.

After respects to the headman, we sat on the earth near the back, exciting titters from the audience and an introduction of "Tuan from America Embassy." I (now referred to as Tuan, an honorific like "Don" in Spanish) then proceeded to address the assembly, wishing them every happiness in the coming year on behalf of President Bush and the entire American people, including Jerry Garcia, who would be arriving in a few days to bless them with gifts of music.

None of this was understood, but it was nevertheless digested politely as an appropriate greeting. Someone said something about Wolfowitz, the former U.S. ambassador, and everyone nodded approvingly and smiled. As the show went on, the acid revealed to me spirits in the trees, weird figures with overgrown snouts and long limbs, much like the puppets themselves, looking down over this village and keeping it safe from harm. I perceived them to be good and gentle spirits, but nonetheless strong guardians of what existed here, and capable of keeping evil spirits out of the village altogether.

Toward dawn the show subsided and Parto and I boarded our trusty jeep and headed west again, like Quixote and Sancho, leaving the village to titter about funny Tuan from American Embassy, the spreader of goodwill.

As the morning blossomed, my acid trip subsided, and I could converse. Parto had been a good companion. He knew that I had been high on something, and he had defended our craft from all threats, real and imaginary.

At noon on Saturday, we hit the coast at Carita, had a swim and a beer, and wound our way back to Jakarta, on familiar roads, and in familiar state of mind.

Chapter Fifteen

I had expected to find the old Dutch house a mess when I came home, but it was quite the contrary. Agustina was on her way back from Bandung, but she had commissioned a major clean up of the place from Parto's wife and another woman. Even Stretch's abode in the guest room looked presentable.

There was still plenty of vacation time yet, Christmas having been celebrated on the road, and we began to plan the New Year's Party of the Year, in Bali. It was a late start, but there were enough people on hand with no plans that it was possible.

I got an inspiration and phoned Saleh, inviting him to meet us at the Hotel Hijau in Legian. There was just no turning back on this thing at this point, and it seemed appropriate to invite the guy. Besides he was cool and he really fit in with our crowd, Iraqi, Lebanese, whatever. I was also wondering how this cool guy was getting along with Larry, who could be charming in a way, but Saleh wasn't turning out to be any normal diplomat of any nationality, not to mention Iraqi. He was complex and interesting, likeable and pretty funky all the way round. He had even managed to take Snake Woman off the market; she hadn't been seen in the bars for weeks.

Larry was back in Ohio this week, trimming his Christmas tree. I figured he would come back to Jakarta with great new ways to promote his career and recruit the Iraqi. I just wondered how far he was going to get.

I was still keeping silent about everything, and just playing things naturally. With some time away from the embassy, I was partly going native and forgetting about my job and its weird accompanying obligations, and partly beginning to worry that this wasn't going to provide an income for too much longer if the polygraph operators and lifestyle security people got hold of me, which no doubt they would sooner or later.

It seemed reasonable to think I could make a living somehow in Indonesia, where I spoke the language and had some contacts, but the business community was very similar to the official community, and I wondered how well I would end up fitting in with them. So it was better not to think too much on these matters, but to take it one day at a time and hope that some divine intervention would make things work out for the best, like everyone always goes around saying it will. I confess that it didn't seem likely.

The group transported itself to Bali by bits. Agustina and I flew, and we stayed with Bina and Candy in the same house in Legian. Kamal took a suite at the Hotel Hijau. He would be host of the party. I had brought my board, and we got some waves for a few days and made preparations. Saleh left a message at the Hijau that he would be in on New Year's Eve, with his fiancée. Islam allowed men to have up to three wives, if they could afford it. Wow, good for Snake Woman, was the general thought, even for Stretch, whose good nature didn't allow him to hold a grudge. Besides, he was now quite interested in Bina, who could put a roof over his head as well as provide other comforts.

We didn't have to lift a finger to make arrangements for the party. It was being done by the hotel, which was laying out a table in a gazebo down by the beach, in a grove of palms that led out to the sand. Lamps and speakers for the music were being strung in the trees. Candy would sing for part of the evening, and we would have house music and whatever we wanted for later. I, of course, brought some of my own selections for a particular point in the evening, and then I laced the punch bowl with LSD, courtesy of Sweeney.

The party kicked off at dusk. We sat in the glow of the evening and the glory that is Bali, and we waded in the surf and chatted as dinner came out. It was a Rijsttafel of sorts, which, in Bali, means it is served by several people carrying out plates of food in file. It is not as ornate and formal as it would have been in Java, which seems appropriate considering the Balinese had chosen suicide over Dutch rule. It was wonderful food with spices and sauces from *rendang* to *padang*, and beautifully prepared and presented by Balinese girls of varying heights, none more than five feet tall.

Saleh and Snake Woman arrived, Snake Woman glistening into the party, enjoying her new-found stature, and wearing a string of pearls that looked fairly genuine. We all exchanged embraces, and our distinguished "Lebanese" guest took his lady through the line. We all helped ourselves to dinner, which lasted until about eight p.m. Then dessert and punch were served.

I quickly moved to the table and took control of serving the punch, making sure the amounts consumed were appropriate to body weight, and that it went all the way around. I then accidentally-on-purpose spilled the punch bowl onto the sand, closing the circle to those present. There is a method to administering this concoction, which is part of the arcane science of my particular strain of California culture, and I knew Sweeney's brand of product from previous experiences in Northern California. We were not original in our use of these pharmaceuticals, but the heirs of a great tradition that flourished in California some years ago. Let's just call it one version of chemical warfare.

Liftoff began around nine p.m. For me there was a pleasant lightening, and a blending with Agustina, whose thoughts I began to read, just as she could read mine. She knew about the punch, and had been preparing herself for this experience, which I would supervise. The rest of the group was unaware. I watched them talking and smiling more as the evening wore on, stopping to gaze and point things out to one another. The mix was right—a soft, kindly acid trip, the trippers unaware. Soon everyone began to dance and hold hands, the food went ignored, and what shoes had been worn were removed.

I looked down on the sand and saw Saleh massaging his woman's feet as she stroked his hair. Both of them were smiling and speaking in low tones to each other, spirits no doubt blending into one another. Again good spirits blessed the event. I saw them in the trees; I recognized one or two from the village, smiling down protectively. A happy mood prevailed.

You had to wonder what people thought was happening to their states of mind, but in practice it never seemed to arise, the trip taking them into its confidence by waves, and concern vanishing as the experience grew. By now everyone had to know they had been drugged, but no one seemed to care. People were laughing and trying to get their thoughts across to one another, high and giggling, stammering and stooping over with laughter.

By the time midnight made its way around the globe to Bali, the party was in full swing: Snake Woman belly-dancing, Saleh providing insights into the greatness of Allah, Stretch massaging Bina's shoulders, and the Aussies dancing circles in the sand with their dates. Agustina and I reclined in a hammock in the palm-studded clearing. A Balinese procession marched through the clearing to the sea, women toting packages on their heads. I would never know if this really occurred or if we imagined it in our altered state of consciousness. At any rate, we both saw it and admired it together, and if it didn't really happen, it should have. The night slipped into oblivion eventually, and we slipped into 1991.

Chapter Sixteen

On New Year's day, the group lounged about in Legian in various stages of hangover. I had an early surf, then we strolled on the beach and slept in hammocks in the shade through the heat of the day. It was a beautiful way to begin a year. Some comments surfaced about the trip of the night before, but nothing was certain except that it had been an extraordinary party, and a uniformly positive experience.

    The holiday season ended suddenly after the new year was welcomed. Saleh went off on a tour of the island with Florida, as she was now called, and people began to drift away, back to Jakarta. We stayed on another day, but the feeling of the event was gone, and we too boarded the plane to Jakarta.

    Things in the Station were now pretty bad. I was lower in the hierarchy than ever, and just pulled myself along in the anticipation that something would break. We were hearing rumors about a potential attack of Iraq to liberate Kuwait, but it was just rumor, and no confirmation came from Headquarters, just talk. I was feeling miserable, wishing I had taken more time over the vacation to travel, and wishing I was far away from the embassy compound and its pasty-faced, middle class, hyper conventional occupants. Every day I would drag myself in, say hello to everyone with a force of will, and try to sound cheerful when I said good morning to Larry, with an extra surge of energy that would nearly tire me out.

I sat through another staff meeting listening to Larry brief the Station about how well his operation was going. It sounded like a briefing he could have written before he left for Christmas. He knew the key to getting ahead, and that was to pre-empt any trouble by anticipating the responses of his listeners and to make his presentation conform to what he thought they wanted. He was safe in Jakarta after all his the years there, because he knew the players and could get his agenda past them. God help him if someone capable took the helm, I thought hopefully, but hope was dim indeed, as no changes in staffing were likely at this time of year.

I could see how Larry and Stokes would have gotten along great, playing golf and softball and looking like they were doing great stuff, and giving briefings in staff meetings about how successful they were going to be. But I reckoned I wasn't much different. I was also doing what I wanted to do, overlooking the mission in favor of surfing and chasing girls around the bars. I guess we are all just what we are in the end, but they could have been friendlier.

The rumors of an American attack to liberate Kuwait were coming on stronger every day. There were warnings to Americans to leave Indonesia unless they were essential to business or other American interests; presumably "essential" included the CIA, so we stayed and watched as the demonstrations began in front of the American Embassy.

Then one morning I came to work and noticed my colleagues had generously dropped the newspaper off on my desk. I thought that was a friendly gesture until I looked carefully at the photo on the front and saw that I was in it. More papers piled up on my desk all day, delivered with smirks by my colleagues. Then the Station Chief called me to his office and gave me a stern lecture about staying out of the front page of the newspaper. Larry sat with a concerned face, not saying a word but holding two copies of the newspaper. Just from that I knew I wouldn't be sitting there had it not been for Larry. Why else would he have two copies if it weren't to show the Station Chief how I had screwed up?

The fact was that the Suara Pembaruan photographer had been covering a demonstration against U.S. intervention in the Persian Gulf while I was walking in the embassy front gate, and his camera caught me looking over my shoulder in my little Brooks Brothers suit, coming back from a secret meeting. To this day if you look up in the archives of Suara Pembaruan from 15 January 1991 you'll find that photo, sure as rain.

There was another problem that set me back a bit further on the Station roster. The very next day we learned that war had broken out and the United States was bombing the crap out of Baghdad. From the snack bar behind the embassy we watched as Wolf Blitzer and others ducked as bombs and missiles hit other parts of the city. Almost everyone knows more about what happened over there than I do, and I knew almost nothing about it then. In fact, it took us completely by surprise, which proves we didn't manage the war from the embassy like most people in Indonesia probably thought. (You have to admit it was a well run war.) What I didn't think of at the time was the effect it would have on our new buddy, Saleh.

We were in the bars as usual, waiting for the next break to get us out of Jakarta. In Betty's Place, we had come up with the idea of pooling our money to get a boat and we were discussing the endless possibilities this would open up to us. A boat would give us access to the Java Sea, and the Pulau Seribu (Thousand Islands) to the north of Java, snorkeling and scuba diving, and a moving party on the bounding main. We had acquired a chart of the region and were trying to figure out distances. We had already researched vessels that might be available in Jakarta. I was for a sailboat, but the general consensus was that they were too slow.

I happened to look toward the billiard tables and saw a fantastically round female bottom from behind, whose owner was racking up a game. Snake Woman was back and looking a bit rough. She was high and her overall appearance was a return to sluttiness. At first, she wouldn't speak to us, but I persuaded her that we were sympathetic by stuffing a twenty dollar bill in her fist. She glanced at it; filed it away in her shirt.

Then we all sat around while Snake Woman told us the effect the war was having on her dude.

It must be humiliating to have a leader who is perceived around the world as an asshole. I guess we Americans should be familiar with that feeling, but for us there is the insulation of being a mega-culture in addition to being an annoying superpower. We have loads of lovable icons to throw around if someone doesn't like George Bush, or Reagan, or Clinton or whomever. When they say that, we just pull out Mickey Mouse, or Jimi Hendrix, or Mohammed Ali, or Levi's, and the speaker has to confess that something good does come out of the U.S.A. When your main face man blunders along brutally killing people and crapping on everything good, then gets his ass kicked for it, and you are still scared to death of him, yet probably feeling a bit of nationalist pride, you throw out your girlfriend and you turn away from your friends and go into hiding. This all made good sense and it was understood by all hands that this is what was going on with Saleh, who now sounded about as Lebanese as Custer.

Snake Woman, being always alert to advantage, went on a little too long about how sad he was, and got another twenty bucks out of it, which I slipped to Stretch so he could deliver it to her. Everyone knew this was his big chance. We call that the fortunes of war.

Then I got my inspiration, and started in. I said one fact was being overlooked in all of this. In California we have a strict tradition that when your world is in a mess, and you have kicked your girlfriend out for bad reasons, and the United

Surfing the C.I.A.

States is bombing your hometown back to Moses, there is only one thing to do: go surfing. No one present had ever set foot in California but me, so they were not in a position to offer evidence to the contrary, and thus no one argued. So it was decided that we would kidnap Saleh and get him into some waves. It was deemed unwise for me to make the approach, being CIA and all, and so it would have to come from Kamal. Once we got Saleh out of town, he would feel much safer. Even Stretch was willing to forego having his big time with Snaky to help out a bro, which was admirable on his part.

It was almost the weekend anyway, and, it being wartime, we decided to all be sick on Friday and make it a long one. We prepared to depart on Thursday night. We got all the boards and beer and everything ready and loaded on my Land Cruiser, Kamal's and the *vehiculus magnus*. Snaky had cheered up, sobered up and showered by this time, and was looking more hopeful, if not her usual sassy self. Kamal stopped near Saleh's house and made the call. The idea was to lure him out in the usual way we do with Iraqis, which is to tell them there are girls outside drooling for a big Arab Johnson, but as Kamal told us afterward, something in Saleh's voice informed him that this was not the time for girls or jokes. Kamal came running back to the cars, which were parked around the corner, and jumped in with me, while Stretch moved over to drive his jeep.

"He told me that he had company, and would like to see me soon, but it sounded very strange," Kamal said. Just then we saw Saleh's car pass us in the opposite direction with him in the back seat and two other people in the front. Saleh looked at us but made no sign as the car swept him along. There was only one course of action open to us, to give chase.

We spun our vehicles around, nearly colliding several times, as the narrow road required much backing up and moving forward, and for several moments we created our own private traffic jam. Thence we finally deployed, although it was several blocks before we caught up, and even then they were onto another street. We were in the Central Jakarta neighborhood of Menteng, where many of the diplomats had their residences. Kamal pulled a handheld radio out of his pocket, snatched his pistol out of his boot, signaled Stretch to slow up alongside, then screamed instructions to him as to how to work the car's CB radio to communicate between the two vehicles. On this one occasion the *vehiculus magnus* was inferior, as it was not wired for CB, so the Aussies pulled up the rear.

The next half hour was a confused maze of transmissions aimed at trying to guess the trajectory of the target vehicle. Kamal would scream "There they are!" and Stretch, having much outback experience in Jackaroo radio decorum, would tell him to calm it down and provide grid coordinates. Much joking and less than serious palaver was exchanged, which didn't help our cause.

Finally we drew a bead on them and got an "eye car" system going, whereby one car would take the lead while another went ahead and tried to anticipate the route. We seemed to be going nowhere after a while. We had never left Menteng, and we had not even broached out onto Jalan Sudirman, when suddenly the Iraqi car slowed to a crawl. This raised a lot of screaming into radios in both Land Cruisers as Stretch tried to double back and get into the action, and the Aussies behind us, without a radio, wondered what the fuck was going on. I was also wondering what the delay was. I finally realized where we were when I looked over my shoulder and saw the great seal of the United States. We were passing by the U.S. ambassador's residence at three miles per hour.

Now, everyone was silent. Everyone but Stretch that is, who wasn't back to us yet. Kamal wasn't answering him on the CB, and he kept asking, "What's happening? What's going on?" It dawned on us then that our recent route through Menteng had been contained in the area of the Ambassador's house, and that we had seen it now from side, back, front, next street over, side, other side, etc. until we had studied the place from every angle, and now, only at the very end, had we driven by the front. I never would have put this together had I not looked up and seen the seal.

The Iraqis now sped up and moved out of the area. We kept on them, driving our clandestine bright red jeep with the boards on the roof, standard issue surveillance vehicle.

They arrived back at Saleh's house. He got out, without a word to them, and they pulled away abruptly. He looked after them, and was still gazing in their direction when we pulled up and hustled him into the jeep. He hesitated an instant, then leaped in. We headed for Betty's Place to hunker down. In the car Kamal handed him the transmitter, and Snake Woman aka Florida spoke to her lover from the other ride.

Chapter Seventeen

Our dude was pretty upset. He explained how he was called to his embassy and instructed by his ambassador to show these visitors around. They only wanted to see one place, and that was Menteng. Over the course of their conversations, they were pretty open with the fact that they were military assassins and were planning to kill American ambassadors wherever they could. Jakarta was their first stop in Southeast Asia, and they would be proceeding to other locations.

    Saleh had played along with them even though he didn't want anyone to get killed, because there was nothing else he could do and if he exhibited the least hesitation he would bring himself under suspicion. Someone asked if we were putting him in danger now, and whether those guys would have any way of following him. He said that they were so stupid that he would be surprised if they could find their way back to their hotel, that they hadn't even noticed they were being followed by three cars full of surfers.

Everyone was silent for a minute as Saleh put away a beer, but the air was pregnant with one universal thought: "They're stupid, that means we can stop them." So the surf trip was off, and the evening was spent in Betty's Place, drinking Bintangs, playing Snooker, and laying out plans to save the ambassador, Saleh, and the world.

For several days, nothing happened. We designated a meeting place, well, Betty's Place in Blok M, for our next installment, which meant someone had to be there every night in case Saleh came in with information. We figured it was better not to use the phones, as the Americans might be tapping them, which worried me, since I didn't want to figure in this in any particular. By way of preparation, we strapped a bicycle to the back of the jeep, and Stretch got a skateboard and put a motor on the back. This was an inspiration to Elvis, who worked two days to build a go-kart, just for the hell of it.

So momentarily, the world went its dismal way, and I started to get a glimpse of others in the Station whose careers might not be as satisfactory as they would have liked, and I began to feel an increasing empathy for disappointed adults who see that other roads are closed to them, and out of desperation hold themselves to the path they chose, day after dismal day, hoping for a break in the weather until retirement, illness or death.

It was pretty depressing but gave me one satisfaction—that I was basically following my own bliss, doing what I wanted to do, if not within my career, then certainly outside of it, no regrets over what I was up to, but ennui in the day job, like the rest of my species.

The person who inspired most empathy at the moment was Krebs. It seemed that his Iraqi operation was a bit of a fudge, and the guy hadn't been keen on getting together with him anymore. Larry claimed that his was going strong, but since he was supposed to be reporting on Saleh, and I had my own eyes into that guy's world, I just could not get the two to jibe. If Saleh was meeting with him at all, he wasn't telling us about it. On the other hand, if Saleh were meeting and providing intelligence, his first report would have been about the assassins who were in town. It was a bit confusing, so I dropped thinking about it by and large, and only gave it passing attention after that.

Fortunately, other matters were arising to occupy my attention. The first was Agustina's announcement that the rabbit died. I did a quick calculation and figured she got pregnant during the luau at the beach. We would have to arrange to go to a clinic, otherwise I would be sent home for sure. At the same time, Sally phoned from Singapore to announce she would be dropping in to visit and "define our situation." This sounded more ominous, as though it might entail some candor and responsibility, and therefore filled me with terror and anxiety. I really liked her, but, well, it was just hard to explain and I will leave it to the reader to judge me innocent or guilty of whatever sin this involves. I didn't want to make a commitment to her, but I didn't want to disappoint her either, and I kind of wished there were some third avenue of emotion to stumble down. I knew this was not the most forthright approach, and that gave me pangs of guilt, but I just couldn't bring myself to bust up with her, dump her, or whatever you want to call it, and on the other hand I couldn't marry her, and besides, Agustina was preggers.

So I waited while the clock ticked, and we waited to see what the Iraqis would do, and meanwhile we were just knocking the crap out of Baghdad. American and coalition forces were attacking from across the desert rather than from the Gulf. Schwartzkopf was in command, Wolf Blitzer was ducking bombs, the Indonesians were protesting, and Saddam was on TV with a little kid who was considered a human shield. The whole Gulf war hype came in on us through CNN and the BBC as we gathered to watch the screens at Top Gun and Betty's Place.

The Station was in a frenzy of unproductive busywork in response to the crisis. Larry reported that he was confident of a recruitment soon, and that intelligence reports about Saddam Hussein's intentions for Southeast Asia would be forthcoming.

Meanwhile, our gang waited for something to happen. We all had ideas, but none of the plans seemed to make much sense in light of the fact we didn't know what the other guys were going to do, so we judged it better to wait and get the benefit of that detail.

Any ideas we had of pulling off anything with any kind of style to it, that is, any romantic notions of doing the thing with a bit of dash and daring, went right into the ashtray. We were pretty scared and not really in any mood to be cool, at least not me. In fact this was a kind of turning point for me and I had a few things I needed to think over, so I got good and stoned one night that week and wound up in bed with two girls I had seen together at the Tanamur.

When we got home they got so into each other they nearly forgot about me, which gave me a chance to think about the operation, but then they became nice and apologetic and included me in the goings on, more than making up for their oversight, for which I was grateful because it gave me a minute to feel like king of the land. They say no plan survives contact with the enemy, and that was certainly the case that night. Any hope of thinking I had, went right out the window once the twosome turned into a threesome; and here I had thought they were queer.

When it came, things began to happen too fast for the eye to follow. First thing we knew, the Iraqi visitors were moving around town and splitting up, so it was the devil to follow them in our surf-wagons. Several times, we had to reduce ourselves to smaller vehicles to keep up. Stretch became very familiar with Menteng on his motorized skateboard, and even though Elvis was keeping the go-kart for more important matters, he wound up deploying it a few times just to make sure it ran. What better place to test a go-kart than in the neighborhood where the quality live? So he would go tearing through the blocks, avoiding the Baby Benz cars and diplomatic license plates. The servants would ward him off and dogs would chase him away, but he had that thing so souped up he would get away and be around the block in no time.

We ended up spending a lot of time in Menteng watching for what we thought was coming, which was some kind of a hit by the assassins, where they would snatch the ambassador from his sleepy guards and kidnap him or shoot at him from some high building close by.

Nothing of the sort happened for two weeks, and my *ménage a trois* hadn't garnered me any insight beyond impatience for the next one, so we kind of relaxed. Stretch started conducting his surveillance with a girl from Tambora in the car with him, and Elvis crashed the go-kart into a tree and bent an axle. It still ran, but it rose up and down as it limped along and only got about 20 mph after that. You have to remember it was hot as well, and we could not be blamed for the natural elements, namely heat and humidity, which nearly cost us our entire enterprise.

Chapter Eighteen

I was thinking it was a shame that the sailboat plan had not gotten further when the phone rang. It was Stretch, stammering and excited about "movement." I understood, got in the jeep and headed toward Menteng. It seems Saleh had been unable to get their complete trust, and the hit team had moved without him. There was a weak point in the perimeter of the ambassador's complex, and the Iraqi car had slowed at that point on several circles around the place. The car had parked there, and for several hours the team had peered over the fence and then removed themselves, later to return to the same spot and peer again. They appeared determined to deploy from this spot, and their repeated visits seemed to confirm this.

Stretch had done enough zooming by on his skateboard now, and more might cause them suspicion, so we got the go-kart back in action. After taking some sledge hammer shots at the axle it moved passably well, although it hiked up on the starboard side a bit, making for a bumpy ride. Elvis took the eye. The Iraqis didn't seem to pay any attention to these small motorized vehicles; probably they were more on the lookout for an official-looking car. Besides it was evening, prime time for Menteng youth to be acting up, and it seemed almost natural for a pony-tailed whoever to be skidding by in a half-cocked go-kart, seeing as they had spent the day being buzzed by a skateboarder whose intelligence connections were laughable. So the lads kept up the vigil until I got to the scene, not that I had much to add.

But I did add this. Instead of traipsing into the ambassador's complex, where we knew there was security, I reckoned we should go around the side of the house (our peep-hole in the wall was at the back), and sneak through to gain a vantage point to watch the bastards from.

It ended up being easy-peasy anyway. We went right over the wall, no dogs, and then we could stop buzzing them in the go-kart, which was starting to list badly to port anyway, and could have wiped out and caused an embarrassment soon. Once we struck a path everyone followed, and we might have handed popcorn around the way we watched those buggers the next two hours from behind that wall. My, but they were patient.

For a full three hours they sat, watching the boss's house while we watched them. I actually fell off and drowsed awhile. When the movement came, one of them went over the wall carrying a parcel. We figured they had kept an eye on the guards and were going through between shifts or so, like they do in escape movies. We didn't know what the fuck to do so we sat still. Eventually, the one guy came back over the wall. Oddly, he took his time getting back to the car. I figure an American would be like, "Let's get the fuck out of here!" but this guy was like, "Well, what else we got in the trunk?" and shit, and they took forever moving on.

When they finally did, we moved in to where they had been. First we took ten minutes, in case they would come back, and even after that we were discreet and stuck to the shadows. I said we should stick to the shadows and keep it quiet while we figured out our plan, but next thing, here comes Stretch on the damn skateboard, his engine whining and winding out into fifth gear. He was yelling for us to scatter, which we did. It wasn't the Iraqis, however, but the ambassador coming home. That scared the crap out of us and it took us awhile to regroup.

Once that racket quieted down around midnight, we had a powwow and decided it was essential for someone to go in. I should say this was a generally shared opinion among us, but there was little agreement as to whom that someone should be. I was a prime candidate, and had I been running for president among the group I could have been elected then and there. It was my belief, however, that Elvis and all his military experience was our shining knight in this hour of need, and that, well, he was the better man. The better man had a response prepared, however, and it was simply that any non-American found on the ambassador's property would be in much more hot water than a CIA guy, who would be presumed to be there for the good of the country. This was a problem for me, because it made good sense, and yet could easily signal the end of my career. There was no doubt the Station would tell the ambassador I was there on official business, but then I would have to face my own bureaucracy, God help me. In the end, however, this opinion prevailed. I saw that since this was my ambassador, nobody else was happy risking their careers, even as a trash-man, to save him, so I went over the wall and began to low crawl across the grass.

One thing that had never occurred to me before is how many crawly creatures live in an Indonesian lawn. I mean it looks benign enough, just like a lawn in Pasadena or Bethesda, but you remember, as you are low-crawling, where you are. I imagined more creatures than Sir Raffles—who catalogued the plants and animals of the East Indies in the 1800's—ever discovered on that thirty yard crawl. Fortunately, about that time, I discovered a trail (yes, crawlers leave a trail, ask any baby) that had been left by the Iraqi assassin. It worked like this: grass resistance was higher to the left, so I went right. When it became more resistant on the right, I went left, and thereby, serpentine, I followed the former traveler's path. My path was so precise that I was headed directly for the patio, or screened-in porch, which faced the lawn. This was the kind of side yard. The back housed the pool, and there was less light over there than elsewhere. Up ahead it got all kind of dark and shadowy. I headed for the shadows via the path of least resistance, shall we say, and when I got there I huffed and puffed and tried to gather my thoughts.

Anyone who has led a life of trouble can imagine my state of mind at this point. I was sorely exposed to problems, I mean how in the hell could I ever explain this if I were found out now; and yet I had my buddies watching me, which meant I couldn't just quit and get out of it. I decided to just sit there for a while, which was fortuitous, as a gardener or watchman or somebody, it could have been the ambassador himself or George Bush for all I knew, came strolling by just about then as though he were playing nine holes. I squeezed in up under the porch and hugged the ground and the shadows like a trembling rabbit, or like Steve McQueen trying to get out of the Gulag. But then, like most things, that problem passed and I had still to figure out what to do. Thanks to that move, I was now up against a kind of a parcel, which had some cloth on it, and had just about the heft and weight of what that Iraqi had brought here. Before I knew what was up I was running with the parcel back to the wall.

Chapter Nineteen

Once over the fence, I stood for an instant, hoping to catch my breath so we could decide what to do. I was for disarming this bomb or whatever it was and letting someone know about it now the danger was behind me. The spot where it had been placed was under a kind of porch, where nobody was at this time of night, so either it was meant to go off in the morning, or maybe it was just supposed to be a distraction while something else happened. Either way we had it, and now I began to unwrap it while everyone crowded around, which is not what you're supposed to do with bombs.

We didn't get far because we heard whistles and the security guys were coming from inside the compound, and there we were standing with a bomb in our hands. Elvis got it straight first, realizing our situation. He grabbed the parcel from me and put it in the go-kart. He pulled the throttle, and the thing took off swerving away down the street. Its goofy wheel made it keep veering to the left until it veered right up on the curb and flew out into the canal.

We watched it land, and by that time the Indonesian security guys were there and they watched it too. They were very sympathetic with us about having lost our go-kart in the canal, and, seeing we were not up to anything more, they went back to their posts.

We figured we still had to keep watch anyway. It could have been their plan to do something to the ambassador or his family while the bomb was going off, so we had better be there to prevent it, or at least to goof up their plan. The rest of the night, we sat in vigil around the place, just keeping an eye out. We watched the sun rise, and eventually we could see people moving around inside the house. Sure enough, the spot where we found the bomb was where everybody gathered to have coffee and mush, and while we were sitting there looking with binoculars into these people's porch, we suddenly heard a sound like a giant belch, way down the street behind us. We looked back and saw that the canal had exploded and was sending mud forty feet in the air. We figured the device had a timer on it after all, and we did good by getting it out of the way. The Iraqis never showed, so we decided the bomb was the thing, and went off to get some sleep.

But that was not to be. When I got home, Sally was there, asleep on the sofa, and I had to do something with her because this was the day I had to take Agustina to the clinic. Stretch and I had a conference and he agreed to distract her for the day. I sneaked past her, got some clothes and went back out.

While I was going, my beeper went off. That had never happened before. It meant my agent, Grisham/7, wanted me to meet him at a designated restaurant to provide me with some vital information or tell me he had a health problem, security problem, or something. Unfortunately, the restaurant was on the other side of Jakarta. I changed my plan and went straight over there, well not straight, but by a circuitous Surveillance Detection Route, which just happened to get me coffee and, from a *warung*, or street vendor, some *martabak* (one of those strangely addictive foreign things you dream of for the rest of your life, a *martabak* is like a giant Ritz cracker dripping with molasses and ketchup—an aquired taste).

When I got to him, he was looking sheepish and told me he had dialed my beeper accidentally and there was no crisis, but he could use an advance on his next month's salary. I gave him some money from my own wallet and hauled ass back over to Kebayoran to pick up Agustina.

As I waited for Agustina in the clinic's waiting room, a couple of girls started flirting with me. So I got a phone number from one of them before we hobbled out of that place. This was a sweet deal this doctor had going. All the supermodel giraffe types went to him for their ob/gyn concerns, abortions, what have you, and he, no doubt, had a lot of fun with the patients. You couldn't even hang around the place without practically getting laid.

But it was good to have that over with. I dropped Agu off at her cousin's place and went back to the Dutch house, where Sally and Stretch were getting on gangbusters. I think it helped that she had seen a woman's clothing hanging in my closet. Women can't be trusted to mind their own business. I adjusted quickly to the situation, which was actually a solution for me, and in the evening we all went out to the bars and Sally and Stretch wound up together in the guest room.

The next day I picked up Agu, and she was introduced all around. Sally seemed okay with that and eventually told me she would have backed off had I told her about Agustina. I said that wasn't in my character. So we had a little get-together that evening in the Dutch house and Agu was up and around and everything was fine.

Chapter Twenty

The week wasn't over yet, so I had to endure two more days in the Station, including a speech by Larry on the inner workings of the Iraqi mind and how to develop them into a reporting source, and blah, blah, blah. Saleh had laid low during the bomb incident, which was according to our plan, in case we got caught he should not be around or they would execute him or something. By this time I was pretty sure Larry was full of crap, but then he produced a report given to him from his Iraqi source telling of an Iraqi plot to assassinate the US ambassador. The plot, he said, had been foiled by an unnamed American, who was a hero to his country, but whose identity would not be disclosed. I was turning pretty red, but nobody noticed, and Larry went on to say that he intended to learn more about this American and report on him, and perhaps we could use such a person as a safehouse keeper or in some other way. He said it was probably a former Green Beret or Marine, probably one of his golfing or tennis buddies from the American Club.

On Friday afternoon, I scheduled an early departure. When I got to the old Dutch house, the troops were assembled for review. There were three surf wagons, all with boards on them, several new girls, including the one from the abortion clinic, who had glommed on to Elvis, and assorted bicycles and skateboards tucked into the vehicles. The guys told me we had one more stop to make, by Blok M on the way out of town, so the procession wound its way down to Jalan Pelatehan, where another jeep was waiting, with Snake Woman at the wheel, and a strange looking man next to her. I recognized my wig and glasses from my disguise kit. Saleh smiled out from under the fake mustache, and the procession moved out toward the south.

We got to Pelabuhan in time to check in to the Buana Ayu and catch a late surf on the right break out front. Everyone was whooping and laughing in the water, and Saleh and Snake Woman did their tandem thing in the nice little knee-high waves. Our luau came off smoothly that night. We danced on the sand, had our barbecue, and when the fire began to glow a bit lower, started talking. Things settled down, and a joint went around. It was only then that Saleh told us that he had had some bad news from home: his sister had been killed in the office where she worked in Baghdad.

It seemed we weren't really getting the picture of the war from the side of the victims, and we never did, as there was nobody to speak for them. Everyone could be affected by the government, and it was so brutal and violent at the top that people never bucked it. As long as you were quiet, did your work and were a good Muslim, you could slide by and hope that things would improve. When you lost one of your family, it could be from such a variety of causes that such deaths were expected, even though you never wanted to have it happen to your family.

Nonetheless, we should have thought more about the casualties. It is impossible to hit a regime from the top and not have a lot of the fallout rain down on the common schlocks who work and do their thing day to day and try to live in that country. We watch TV and see how effective our weapons are, and never imagine what it would be like to have them aimed against us. The worst part would be the uncertainty of what kind of attackers are these? Are they going to stop ever, or are they going to kill us all? Or are they going to kill enough of us to make the misery of loss our primary penance?

Imagine a nation capable of wiping out America bombing us and watching it on TV. Are we so brutal that we don't consider the ones we attack to be human beings? Are there not enough casualties on the other side for us to count them as we count our own? When it's someone you know, or his sister who has died, been deformed or permanently maimed by the machine of war, the thing gets personal very fast.

As people drifted away that evening in couples, everyone placed a hand on Saleh's shoulder, and everyone knew who the real hero was. I never asked him about his report to Larry, but it was clear he knew I was American, and our countries were at war with one another. He had just saved my country's ambassador, and my country had killed his sister.

The night waned away into the wee hours, and we didn't go to sleep, but just sat there and said little. I kind of considered it a wake for my friend's sister, and it was unsaid and formal, as though she were there. I didn't want to ask him too much, nor talk too much, and I was ashamed of the destruction of which human beings are capable. I wasn't ashamed of being an American, that was no use and was never going to change. It was humanity that appalled me. I was ashamed of being human.

Snake Woman was asleep with her head on Saleh's lap, and I thought to myself what a man he was to have tamed her. I never could have done it. She would have been off with the next guy in no time, but there she was, that wild party girl, snoring gently and holding on to him with a grip like G.I. Joe.

Stretch bumbled over a couple of times into the light of the campfire, said some awkward things to try to make conversation, then quickly retreated to the comfort of his sleeping bag and Sally. I noticed she held it open for him when he returned to her, and that was okay. I sat there and thought about the abortion. I looked at Agu next to me, the little mother, whose head was in my lap, and I thought next time we'll go ahead and have the kid, career be damned, and I will take this woman to my heart and make her happy. Then, I thought, why stop there. I decided to work against war, and to get out of this business, which engages in it secretly. I thought of Saleh too, who had other thoughts in his heart than revenge on his enemies. After all, he had told Larry that an American had saved the ambassador, not a Brazilian, but I knew that it was neither one of those. We both seemed to stir at about the same time. We reached across and gave each other a handshake, surfer style. Then we hugged each other, knocking the girls' heads together in the process.

The dawn came in kindly, cool and sweet, and the sun rose on a tranquil world, beaming down upon the beach like a benediction. The surf was smooth and glassy, with chest-high waves breaking over the sandbar right out front of the Pasar Monyet in waist-deep water: perfect girlfriend surf. Everyone went in. Saleh and Snake Woman caught waves together on the big board, and people surfed in their Hawaiian shirts and straw hats and played in the waves together, wiping out on top of each other. Somebody cranked up the stereo, the Grateful Dead rocked the sands and the Indian Ocean, and we roasted hot dogs (kosher beef) and had cold beer for breakfast.

Several weeks went by after that weekend at the beach, and Saleh couldn't get away again. The war was over by the end of February, and nothing had changed much in our lives, despite the destruction wrought on the Iraqi people. One night I saw Snake Woman down at the bars by herself. She handed me a short note from Saleh, which said:

"My good friend and brother, I have been summoned back to my country, and until this situation changes I shall not see you again. Please think of me when you are surfing, and I will be thinking of you on the other side of the world somewhere. If I ever hear the Grateful Dead, or attend a luau in the moonlight, I will remember you. Your friend, Saleh."

Back in the Station, Larry reported, accurately, that his contact had been summoned back to Baghdad, but that he was closing in on discovering the identity of the American mentioned in the intel report, and had more details about the attempted assassination of the ambassador, and a bomb that had blown up a canal in Menteng. That was okay, whatever he would find out wouldn't amount to much. In the meantime, we had bought a boat and were planning a trip to an island off the west coast of Java, a hardcore right hand tube.

Chapter Twenty-one

From the eastern sky the sun burned across a shimmering sea and lit the glossy white hull of the vessel as it rocked gently on the swells, pulling at its anchor, well out of danger from the surf, but close enough to paddle to the waves with ease across a blue expanse of water the color of a swimming pool. A sea snake had taken roost in the open transom of the boat, and we couldn't seem to get it to leave, but it wasn't doing any harm, apart from being deadly venomous. It wasn't aggressive, and its black and green bands took the early morning light as it swam just off the stern. Stretch was convinced it was nesting and we would soon have little venomous babies all over the place, and was for killing it, which I forbade, and the girls wouldn't swim near the boat. I knew we would have to do something eventually, but not right away. I threw my board in the water, well clear of the snake, and swam after the board, figuring I had about a ten minute paddle to the empty, perfect waves gracefully tumbling over the reef—thin waves, delicate, feminine.

I was the first one up this morning, and the sun hadn't cleared Sumatra yet. This island was part of the Mentawai chain, and its natives were seldom seen although we knew they were there in the forest. Occasionally we would catch sight of one or two of them, and often we saw a lone man in a dugout canoe far out to sea. Sometimes they would come over to the boat and ask for medicine, and hold onto our lines for half an hour or so, then paddle away, but when we were on the land we never saw them. Anyway, we wouldn't spend much time on the beach, especially at dusk because of the mosquitoes and the malaria.

As I paddled toward the lineup I thought to my trip back to headquarters, from which I had just returned.

There was the strange icy landing at a sullen Dulles Airport and the bare, bare trees, the cutting wind and the yellow taxis around town, the Key Bridge and Georgetown, all grey and solid and made of stone, and the half-frozen Potomac River flowing clean and frigid from its headwaters near Harper's Ferry; bare trees and more bare trees. I passed through Arlington, and by Strangeways, which looked a bit forlorn and stark in the suburban winter scene. I wondered where she was, the girl with the hummingbird on her wrist.

Then I was on the George Washington Parkway, and CIA headquarters loomed into view with its concrete façade lightened up by green windows. The taxi swung onto the ramp and up to the security gate to headquarters, with its famous entrance and star-studded wall and the great CIA seal on the floor in marble.

My week was a rush, crowded with meetings and briefings and medical and so forth, no polygraph or lifestyle inquiries, praise be to Allah. I saw old friends from the Farm and training days whose assignments had taken them elsewhere, or who simply hadn't left.

I had dinners by myself near my hotel, always armed with a book to read, or walked into Georgetown and poked around. In the evenings, I shopped with a list of gifts for people back home. The shopping center at Tyson's Corner was wadded with people and gave me culture shock; I couldn't seem to get a foothold on the society anywhere. Everywhere I went I was a stranger; it was disconcerting to feel so far from home. I had looked forward to being in the States, but when I arrived I couldn't seem to find it.

One evening I dropped into Strangeways, just to have a look and to kind of put a lid on the whole thing, but she was gone, and so were her paintings. The bartender was a guy with green hair and tattoos of women and mandalas down both arms. The visit was over soon, with just one meeting to go.

The ceiling fans whirred nearly noiselessly in the cafeteria, and chubby Americans padded along, stuffing their trays with salads and sushi. I was there to meet a young officer who was interested in coming out to Jakarta, who had heard that I would be in from the field for a week, and who wanted to ask me some questions. He stood up as I approached his table, and stretched out his hand to greet me, very respectfully. As we talked he told me quietly that he was recently engaged, and was hoping his bride would be comfortable in Jakarta, were he to accept the assignment.

She had given him a list of questions about the housing, and they were planning a family, so could I also comment on the sanitation situation. I told him that I could personally say that sanitation in Jakarta was in excellent hands. He also hoped to improve his golf game and understood that Jakarta was an excellent place for golf and he felt it was also a sport that could advance his career, and did I agree?

I told him about the American Club, and its Mongolian barbecues on Sunday nights, and he smiled and told me that he and his wife would be going to Bible study on Sunday nights, but that maybe on Saturdays he could play tennis there, if there were not too much work to do in the office.

He was very interested in the American community, and I told him what little I knew about it, and tried to be helpful and friendly. As we parted, he said "I heard you recruited a North Korean. Congratulations."

I issued the standard denial mandated by Chapter 6 of the CIA Manual, but wondered if I was finally getting credit for something, albeit a twisted and inaccurate set of facts. Maybe Larry was not so intransigent after all.

"Salamat Jalan," I said. Good luck.